D1194334

Writing on the Wall

CHRISTOPHER CLEARY

Immortality Press
Alpharetta, GA

WRITING ON THE WALL

Published by Immortality Press

www.immortalitypress.com

Library of Congress Control Number: 2007927069

ISBN 978-0-9795753-5-8

Book design by www.KareenRoss.com

Editing by Patti J. Daniels

Manufactured in the United States of America

O N E

———————————

Donnie Betts rode his bike nearly everywhere with the exception being school because he was neither in a hurry to get there nor to return home. He preferred the leisurely walk even during the chilly winter months. During the walk, he could be alone without feeling lonely. At home, he could feel lonely even when someone else was there.

"Hey!"

Donnie did not bother turning around to see who was calling.

"Hey, Donnie!" the female's voice hollered again.

Since he was now certain that she was calling out to him, Donnie turned around. As he suspected, it was the new girl. He stopped walking and waited for her.

Donnie had never realized how good a pair of jeans could look until she sauntered toward him wearing Sevens. With each step of her platform sandals, he admired the contour of her legs and marveled at the elegant physics of a person walking. Freckles were splattered across her cheeks and nose like someone had flicked a paint brush toward her face. And her shoulder-length wavy hair was a perfectly blended spectrum of red and blonde that stood out against her white corset while complementing the turtle-green of its lacy overlay.

"I've been going to school here for a week, you know?" she said.

"Yeah?" Donnie didn't understand why she said it like he was in trouble.

"I live right across the street from you."

"I know. I saw you move in."

"If you know, why do you walk home ahead of me every day?"

"Because I leave sooner than you do."

"Instead of walking home with me?" she clarified for him. "Why do you walk ahead of me instead of with me?"

He adjusted his backpack and provided her with a candid response, "It never occurred to me to walk home with you."

"Oh?"

Unlike many teenagers, Donnie didn't rush to say something just to fill up the empty air. It wasn't that he was shy, but when he was around strangers, Donnie chose his words carefully. He looked at the tree branch directly above them and reached up with one of his lanky arms. The cuff of his black, long-sleeved T-shirt slid away from his wrist as he stretched. Donnie plucked an autumn leaf from the tree.

The girl waited for him to speak. When he didn't, she put her left hand to her forehead and then held it out, palm up. "Now that it has occurred to you," she said, "would you like to continue to walk ahead before I start following you again or shall we walk together now?"

Donnie twirled the leaf by the stem. "We can walk together."

"K," the girl said and resumed walking. Donnie did not immediately join her. She didn't stop but instead turned around and, while walking backwards, said to him, "*Walking* together, Donnie. Not *standing* together."

He covered ground quickly with his long legs and was by her side after a few quick strides.

"Do you even know my name?" she asked.

"Heck, I have trouble remembering my own."

She smiled at his remark. Really smiled. It wasn't the counterfeit one she had been using the entire first week at her new school. "Megan," she told him. "Megan Priddy."

"Want me to carry your books?"

"Did you just ask me if I wanted you to carry my books?"

"No. I asked if you wanted to carry my books."

"No, you didn't."

"Then why'd you ask what I asked?"

She genuinely smiled for the second time in under a minute. Her face wasn't accustomed to it. It wasn't that she was opposed to smiling, but the opportunities for it were few in number when moving to a new town and a new school where nothing was familiar. She felt like she was continuously on the outside of an inside joke.

"Why don't you take the bus?" Megan inquired.

"Just don't."

"Why not?"

"It's not that far and I kind of like being alone."

"But it's cool if I walk with you?"

"So far. What about you? Why don't you take the bus?"

"They didn't have buses at my old school." She shrugged just one shoulder. "Some old habits aren't worth breaking."

The agitated bark of a murderous dog sounded off like an unpredicted, sharp crack of thunder. The fence on Megan's left creaked and rattled as the dog slammed its weight against it. Her body went rigid and she stumbled into Donnie. The canine's nails frantically scraped against the rotting wood and its saliva-drenched snarl continued, but Donnie and Megan were safe on the other side.

She exhaled a sigh of relief. "Every day," she said. "That dog scares me every day I walk by."

"You'll get used to it."

"That thing sounds nasty. What kind of dog is it?"

The slats of the fence were too close together to make out the breed.

"I've never seen it," Donnie told her. "Be funny if it was like just a little wiener dog or something like that."

"Sounds like a deranged Wookie."

When they reached their street, Megan asked, "Why'd you carry that leaf all the way home?"

"Oh, um…"

"Are you going to take it inside with you?"

"Yeah."

She meant for her question to be sarcastic, but when he answered with sincerity, she was compelled to ask, "Why?"

Using the hand not holding the leaf, Donnie Betts scratched the back of his head through his wavy black hair. "It's pretty, isn't it?" he asked.

"Yeah."

"It's dying. How many things do you know of that become so pretty when they're dying?"

Megan didn't answer because she couldn't think of any.

———————————

Haviland High wasn't the first new school for Megan Priddy, but she hoped that it would be her last before college. She began her sophomore year in another state but ended up in Haviland, Georgia, a comfortable town 25 miles north of Atlanta.

To everyone who attended Haviland High, she had no past. There weren't any preconceived impressions of her. Her peers would never know that she used to shy away from attention or why.

Donnie was reluctant to wait for Megan when school let out, but she always caught up with him during his walk and scolded him for not being more considerate. After a few days,

Donnie began to hang around at the rear door of the school near the gymnasium for her. He joked that he waited to keep her from complaining about walking alone, but the truth was, he was beginning to enjoy her companionship.

Their commute became a routine. Megan always made him laugh when she poked fun at the silly sayings on New Hope Church's marquee. When they were approaching the Richies's dog with the ferocious bark, Donnie would warn her. And when Megan's homework load was light, they stopped at Swifts for Polar Slurps.

They didn't share any of the same classes and Donnie rarely spoke more than a few sentences during school hours. The majority of their conversations were held on the way home and, even then, large chunks of their walk would pass in a comfy silence.

The fluorescent lights in Haviland High's cafeteria created an overexposed haze above everyone's heads and the aroma was only slightly more appetizing than reheated cat food. For the first week or two at her new school, the combination turned Megan's stomach inside out. Amazingly, she began associating the lighting and the smell with her lunchtime hunger, causing the cafeteria to become an appetizing atmosphere.

Holding her lunch tray in both hands, Megan approached Donnie's table.

"Hey, Donnie."

The six boys, including Donnie, simultaneously stopped chewing their food. It was uncommon for a girl to approach their lunch table.

"I noticed that Swifts has a couple of arcade games," she said. "I've got a bunch of quarters. You wanna stop there on the way home today?"

Donnie didn't reply.

"You know, Swifts?" she prompted. "We stopped there yesterday for Polar Slurps. The convenience store we pass every day? Can we go in again today?"

Again, no reply from Donnie.

One of his lunch companions, who sported a thin and cheesy mustache that was struggling to grow like spring grass without enough rain, looked at her tray and said, "Steamed vegetables? Freshman mistake. Friday is Platypus Pizza Pie day, Priddy. You never want to pass up the Platypus Pizza. And no Popsicle? Double boner."

Bip, a tough, short kid with glasses, read the wrapper of his Popsicle and said, "According to the wrapper, it's actually a 'Delicious Frozen Confection.'"

Megan tightened the grip on her tray to prevent it from slipping. She felt a thin film of sweat forming on her hands and wanted to leave before the boys noticed.

"I'm a little rusty on my mental telepathy, Donnie. So if you could just nod or shake your head that would be helpful."

Donnie's tablemate with the cheesy mustache continued, "They have steamed vegetables everyday. And who eats that crap, anyway? You have to seize the opportunity when they offer something good –"

Donnie's voice was more defined than Megan had ever heard it. "Lay off, Dale," he told cheesy mustache boy.

He turned to face her. The usual tenderness returned to his tone. "I'm in," he said, "as long as you don't mind getting your butt kicked."

Megan puffed a strand of hair away from her face. "You're dreaming."

TWO

Donnie and Megan grew bored with Swifts's two video games before they ran out of quarters, but that didn't stop them from playing until they were all gone. Reluctantly, Donnie pulled on his backpack and Megan hoisted her satchel over her shoulder. It was Friday and neither was anxious to go home early.

"What was your deal at lunch today?" Megan asked. "Why were you ignoring me?"

"I wasn't ignoring you."

The glass door of the convenience store bing-bonged when Donnie pushed it open for them to exit.

"What then?" Megan wanted to know.

"I was thinking."

"Sheesh. How far in advance do I need to ask you to play video games?"

"That's not what I was thinking about."

"What then?"

Donnie was purposely being vague because he didn't want to talk about it. Megan picked up on this, but ignored his reluctance. Donnie was acting strangely and she wanted to get to the bottom of it.

"You never really talked to me at school before," he told her.

"So?"

The sole of his high-top sneakers scuffed the pavement while he carefully considered his response. Donnie avoided speaking if what he had to say left him vulnerable to ridicule. In the end, he figured that he should just lay it on her and get it over with.

He said, "It surprised me. I didn't think – I only thought that you talked to me on the way home from school because I was the only person there to talk to. I didn't think that you'd actually come find me at school. And then, it was cool to know that you were planning something for us to do."

"Oh. That's it?" She stopped walking. He did the same. "K, so now I've talked to you at school, right?" He nodded. "And I blew all the quarters with the different states on them that my grandma sent me on video games with you. Right?"

"Yeah."

"So now you never need to be surprised when I talk to you at school or think that I mean something other than what I'm saying. K?"

Donnie literally breathed easier. It was a relief. They were free to be themselves. Donnie and Megan never had to put on a show for each other.

"Yeah, all right."

She socked him in the arm and they resumed walking at an even slower pace.

"When do you turn sixteen?" Megan asked.

"I am sixteen."

"Do you have your license?"

"Learner's permit."

"That sucks."

"Yeah." Donnie's response sounded indifferent.

Relying on centrifugal force to keep her books from dropping out, Megan twirled her satchel around one time and set it back on her shoulder. "I can't wait until I'm sixteen," she said.

"What for?"

"I want to use the drive-thru."

"What drive-thru?"

"Any drive-thru! I want to pull up and order whatever and then be in the driver's seat to get it."

"You got a thing about other people touching your food or something?"

"It's a freedom thing, Donnie. You understand. Don't be a smart ass."

Donnie smiled. For some reason, he liked it when Megan used cuss words, which wasn't often or it wouldn't have been special. And because he knew that she never meant it in a mean way, he especially liked it when he was the target of the word. "Yeah," he conceded, "I get it."

To battle the onset of dusk, street lights flickered on and stores fired up their marquee lights. The Parkside Storage sign gleamed brighter than Hollywood. Beneath its name, removable black letters advertised a "Renter's Special."

Donnie read it, "'First month only $9.' I wonder how much the rest of the months are?"

Megan got Christmas-morning excited. "We should do it."

"Do what?" Even though he had just read the sign out loud, he wasn't sure what she was talking about.

"Rent a unit."

"I don't have anything to put in it."

Exaggerating exasperation, she explained, "Just like a place to hang out. Somewhere to go other than home."

"We can't."

"Why not?"

The idea of having their own private place to crash intrigued Donnie, but he had a nagging sensation that it wasn't something that they could get away with. "Are you serious?"

"Yeah! And we'd keep it our secret. Just you and me and

no one else. No one." Megan swung around in front of Donnie and lightly pushed him to a stop with one hand. She stared him down with her pineapple-leaf green eyes. The smattering of light-colored freckles across her nose and cheeks intensified. Her enthusiasm added vibrancy to her body. For the first time, Donnie looked past her mesmerizing hair and realized that Megan was a cutie. Covertly, she asked, "You can keep a secret, can't you, Donnie?"

He nodded.

They weren't dating or anything like that. The new girl just happened to move to his street and their personalities meshed like that of sit-com buddies. Donnie could think of lots of reasons why he shouldn't agree to renting a storage unit with her, but he couldn't think of one really good one.

"Can you say it for me?" she asked. "Can you promise me?"

In that moment, Megan Priddy could have asked for anything and Donnie would have agreed. He told her, "I promise I'll keep it our secret."

She laughed and skipped ahead of him before turning around and saying, "Well, come on! We've got planning to do!"

Megan wasn't allowed to have guests inside the house when her parents weren't home, a rule that she could thank her older sister for; however, a loophole existed. The deck on the back of the house was merely attached to it, not inside it. Donnie walked around the side of the house while Megan went through it.

When they reunited on the deck, Megan said, "Usually my parents go out on Saturday nights instead of Fridays." She held up a twenty dollar bill. "They left money for pizza. What toppings do you like?"

"Pepperoni."

She rolled her eyes. "Everyone gets pepperoni. What else?"

"Cheese."

She dropped her head backwards and exhaled as she pulled it forward. "Fine. We'll get it with pepperoni and cheese, but I get to pick the next one."

Megan began punching numbers on the cordless phone before realizing that she was dialing the pizza shop in her old state. "Oh, duh," she said. "I have to get the phone book." She went back inside the house, returned with the telephone book, and sat down at the table with Donnie.

After soliciting his advice on which pizzeria to call, Megan ordered a pepperoni pizza. Then she looked up the phone number to Parkside Storage. "Geez-oh-man," she said. "Did you know there are three of them?"

"I know there's more than one."

"What's the name of that street we walk home on?"

"Memory Lane."

"Really? How quaint." She pointed to the number in the book, "K, here it is."

"What are you going to say?"

She already had the number dialed. Since Donnie could only hear one side of the phone call, Megan's conversation with Parkside Storage sounded like a monologue to him. "Hello... I was calling about your special… How much does it cost after the first month?... I don't know. What sizes do you have?" As the person on the other end was speaking to her, she fumbled through Donnie's backpack for a pen and paper. She grabbed his spiral bound five-subject notebook and opened it. Donnie snatched it back and ripped out a single sheet of paper before returning the notebook to his backpack.

"Do you mail the bills or can I just pay at the office?" Megan spoke into the receiver. "You know, I like to cut back on the use of paper products. Save the trees and all." She shrugged her shoulders and smiled at Donnie. "K. That's all I need right now." Donnie waved at her. "Wait a second…"

Donnie whispered, "How long will the special run?" Megan liked that he was finally taking an active role in their secret project and gave him a thumbs up.

"How long will the special run, sir...K. Well, then…, oh wait!" She thought of something else. "One more question – how old do you have to be?... K. Thanks! Bye!"

Donnie waited silently as she scribbled down a few notes. "Good thing you called," he said. "I'm a lousy note taker."

"What are you talking about? Your notebook is filled with notes."

Donnie changed the subject, "I can't believe you just called Parkside Storage."

"I can't believe that you only have pencils in that back-pack."

Donnie lamely defended his writing utensils, "They're mechanical pencils."

"Nerd," she said, finishing up her notes. "Pens are where it's at. Preferably purple."

"Like I'm going to use a purple pen."

"Pink?" Megan offered with a smirk.

"How do you erase your mistakes?"

"I don't make any."

Donnie reached across the table and turned the sheet of notes so he could read it. "You misspelled 'storage'," he informed her.

"Oops." Megan turned the paper back around. Instead of using the eraser, she scratched it out and rewrote it.

Donnie observed, "That's how you do it."

"Yeah, Donnie," she imitated his post-pubescent deepened voice, "That's how I do it."

It was endearing to see her pretend that she was him. Grinning at her, he said, "Shut up."

"You shut up."

"No, you shut up."

"Do you want to know what he said or what?" Megan asked.

"No." It was a lie and she knew it. Of course he wanted to know.

She tapped the pencil on the table a few times and said, "K. You want something to drink?"

"All right. I want to know. What did he say?"

"I'll tell you after the pizza gets here."

Donnie folded his arms across his chest. Megan smiled and went inside to get a couple of sodas.

As they shared the pizza, Megan said, "We're going to need to get jobs."

"How much is a unit?"

"One-hundred and nineteen dollars after the first month."

"That's not so bad."

"No." The excitement Megan had originally exhibited had disappeared from her tone, but internally she was still buzzing from the idea. "I'll apply at that ice cream shop restaurant place. What's it called?"

"Friendly's?"

"Yeah, that's the one. They had a 'Servers Wanted' sign in the window." She wiped her mouth with a linen napkin and said, "Now what about you?"

"I don't know."

"K, but you promise to think about it?"

"Yeah."

"No freeloading." She wagged her finger at him. "You have to pay for your half."

"All right, Megan. I'll get a job." He took another slice from the box. "What did he say when you asked how old you had to be?"

"Eighteen."

Donnie dramatically dropped the slice of pizza on his plate. "Well, there's no hurry for me to get a job then. It's going to be two years until we can rent it."

She smiled, biting one side of her lower lip as she did. "You find a place to work and leave that to me."

THREE

Donnie Betts walked Megan Priddy to her first day of work at Friendly's.

She didn't have any difficulties landing the job. She was cute, smart, and willing to work for minimum wage. Her interview lasted only ten minutes. All she had to do was flash her fake smile, which everyone fell for, and utter a few intelligent and mature thoughts. She had never been on an interview before, but she didn't consider the questions difficult.

When the manager asked, "What's your work ethic?" the answer was obvious.

"I'm committed to performing tasks in a timely and efficient manner, ma'am."

"Have you ever worked a cash register?"

Megan substituted her every day "fun girl" voice for one that was as adult as she could make it. She also tried to use as many words with more than one syllable as she could conjure. "I haven't had the opportunity to acquire that skill as of yet, but I am an A student and excel in mathematics."

"Have you ever taken down a customer's order?"

"This would be my first server position; therefore, I do not have experience with taking orders. I do, however, have an excellent memory and take plenty of notes at school. I would be dedicated to maintaining Friendly's high standards, and customer satisfaction would be a top priority."

The manager didn't let Megan leave until she agreed to start work on Saturday.

"Here we are," Donnie announced as if Megan didn't realize they were standing in front of the small restaurant and ice cream shop. "You nervous?"

"Hell yeah, I am! It's my first real job!"

She seemed to be playing it so cool that her volatile reaction was startling. "All right. Take it easy. Relax," Donnie prompted her.

"'All right. Take it easy. Relax.' That's all you've got? You ask me a question like that and when I freak, that's what you say? 'Relax?' That's all you've got?"

Donnie held up a hand. "Whoa. You're still freaking out and it's starting to freak me out."

Megan's words shot out like the sharp strikes of a typewriter, "Why are *you* freaking out?"

"You're usually the one who has it together, so when you freak out," the pitch of his voice raised, "I get freaked."

"You can't right now, Donnie. You need to be the rock. You need to be the one to say something good."

"OK." Donnie licked his lips and thought for a moment. "You're the smartest girl I know and renting one of those storage units was a really cool idea. Anyone who can come up with something like that can work at Friendly's blindfolded and wearing earmuffs."

Megan took a breath. "I guess that'll have to do."

He added, "Plus, you look really good in that uniform."

"I do?" Megan thought that neither the plain black pants nor the short-sleeved shirt with thick alternating red and white stripes complemented her figure.

Donnie's broad smile betrayed his sincerity and revealed his jest.

"You jerk," she said and slapped him on the arm. "Go find a job."

Donnie's smile vanished. His face turned somber.

Megan tucked a lock of hair behind her ear. "What is it?" she asked, attempting to ascertain why he suddenly looked offended.

"Don't say that."

"Say what?"

It pained Donnie to speak the words, "'Go find a job.'"

"But you need to."

He was visibly irritated and upset. "I know, Megan."

"I wasn't.... I didn't mean it mean. I just meant..."

"I know." His eyes looked everywhere except at Megan. This bothered her. She felt disconnected from him. Even worse, Donnie appeared disconnected from the world. "Just, if you gotta say it, say, 'seek employment' or 'look for work.' Just not those exact words."

"K." Megan quickly agreed. She didn't like seeing Donnie so distraught. "Do you want to tell me what's wrong?"

He had brought his bicycle along on the walk so he could ride it after Megan went to work. Staring at the seat of the bike, he told her, "You've got to go to work. Some other time, huh?"

"Yeah... All right."

Donnie threw a leg over the bike and took off down the street. He wasn't exceptionally strong, but his lanky body was well-proportioned for bike riding.

He only knew one speed – fast. This helped him clear his mind but prevented him from seeing all of the storefronts. He slowed down enough to start considering some of them as a place where he might find employment.

Without going inside any of the stores, he concluded that there wasn't a good place to work on Memory Lane. The jobs were either unappealing, or if the shop or restaurant was hip, he assumed you had to be a special breed of person to work there.

Starting a new job was also intimidating. A job meant responsibility and responsibility translated into opportunities for failure or making a fool of himself or both.

Tugging at him from the other direction was Megan. He didn't want to let her down. She couldn't wait to find a job and had applied at Friendly's the following day. He wanted to duplicate that excitement of hers and the surest way to achieve it was to get a job and help pay for his part of the storage unit.

Donnie turned down a side street that he normally didn't ride on with the hope of locating a new business that was hiring.

In a short amount of time and distance, the side street became vacated of pedestrians and cars. The road spilled into the woods, splitting them like the part in a person's hair. He had never biked on that road before, but he figured it to be an obsolete route to the next town. That town would be too far to bike several days a week for work, but he was enjoying the journey and had no immediate desire to turn back.

The noon-time heat of the Indian summer, combined with his exhaustion, made Donnie thirsty.

There was a clearing that extended several hundred yards on the left side of the road. At the end of it, nearest the street, was a gravel parking lot. In it sat five cars and a brown rectangular shack with a black saltbox roof. Against its side, shining like the solitary jewel of a tarnished crown, was a soda machine.

The artificial breeze created by his bike cutting through the air was Donnie's only relief from the heat. When he came to a halt in the gravel parking lot, the day's humidity immediately caught up with him. Perspiration covered his face and his shirt began to stick to his body.

There was the sound of golf clubs smacking golf balls, but he knew that it wasn't a golf course. He purchased his soda and walked around the shack. A bunch of guys were lined up in a row and hitting golf balls into the open field. It was a driving range, where golfers practiced their swing.

Donnie, trying to cool down before resuming his search for employment, sipped his soda and took in the scene.

"Come here!" the man from inside the shack called to Donnie. His natural voice sounded like it was being projected from a drive-thru speaker.

Using the hand that was holding the can of soda, Donnie extended his index finger and held it against his chest.

"Yeah, you," the man said, slightly annoyed that he had to specify even though no one else was standing around the kid.

Donnie walked up to the long rectangular window of the shack. He spotted a half-eaten box of doughnuts next to the man who wore a baseball cap that looked like it had been buried by a dog. Hair stuck out of every part of his body that was exposed. It grew on his face, fled from his nose, and extended from underneath his hat. Hair poked out of two or three quarter-sized holes of his brown T-shirt like weeds growing through a crack in the driveway. Where his short sleeves stopped, a layer of hair covered his arms all the way down to the middle of his fingers.

"How old are you?" he demanded.

"Sixteen."

"You here to hit golf balls?"

"No. I stopped for a soda." He held up the can as proof.

A neatly dressed golfer asked for another bucket of golf balls. The hairy man in the shack charged him five dollars and told the buyer to help himself to any of the buckets on the counter.

"You're tall for sixteen," he said once his attention returned to Donnie.

Donnie considered the meatball-shaped man to be short for whatever age he was, but when he asked, "You need a job?" Donnie thought of him as some type of fallen leprechaun angel serving penance at a driving range.

Donnie scratched his cheek and inquired, "Doing what?"

"'Doing what?'" the man said, making sure that he heard the words right. "'Doing what?'" he repeated in disgust. "What's your name?"

"Donnie Betts."

"Donnie, they call me Dirt. Turn around." Donnie was hesitant to do so. The man leaned forward on the counter. The sharp pitch of his voice crackled, "Ain't nothin' goin' happen to ya. Turn around."

Donnie did as he was told.

"You see all them golf balls out there?" Dirt asked. Donnie nodded. "I need you to pick them balls up." Donnie continued to stare upon the open field well after Dirt finished speaking. "Turn back around!" Once Donnie was facing him again, he continued, "There's a lot of them, huh?" Donnie nodded again. "I'll give you two cents a ball for every one you pick up. No. Wait." He reconsidered. "I don't want to count all them damn balls. I've pay you four-fifty an hour, under the table." Donnie's face crinkled in confusion. "You don't know what 'under the table' means?"

"No." It was the first word Donnie uttered since he had told Dirt his name.

"Means the government gets none of it. I'm paying you less than the minimum wage," his voice lowered and sounded somewhat menacing, "which we won't tell nobody about, right?"

Donnie didn't understand exactly why, but he knew that he better respond in the affirmative. "Right."

"But even so, you'll still make more than you would after the government taxes the shit out of it. We both win. Comprendé?"

"I get it."

"Step around the side here." Dirt disappeared out of sight.

Donnie walked around to the side of the brown shack. Dirt opened the door and lowered a baseball helmet on Donnie's head. It was so large and loose that it rattled any time Donnie moved. Dirt threw an empty newspaper bag over Donnie's shoulder and handed him a stick with a scoop and small basket on one end.

"Careful," Dirt cautioned. "Them balls sting if you get hit."

FOUR

It did not take Megan long to find her groove at Friendly's. Since she was one of the younger employees, the manager usually scheduled her to work the ice cream window. Once winter swept in, sales from the outside window slowed. This provided Megan with more opportunities to work as a server inside the restaurant. The servers at Friendly's did not make the largest tips, but it was a decent sum for a fifteen year old.

Donnie's job required much less brainwork. He simply had to fill the newspaper bag with golf balls and return them to the shack, a process that he repeated numerous times during a shift.

There was a lot of open space where the golf balls might fly, so the probability of being hit was low. He also avoided working during the busiest times to lessen that chance even more. In the six weeks that he worked there, it only happened once. And Dirt was right; it did sting.

A man hollered "Fore!" Without thinking, Donnie turned to look. That wasn't the smartest move because he was exposing his face. He saw the hard white ball headed straight for his noggin. He backpedaled away from the tee boxes, but it was hard to move quickly carrying a full bag. The golf ball nailed his foot on the fly. The foot bruised and he limped for a week, but it healed with time and no permanent damage was done.

Whereas Megan received a paycheck every two weeks, Donnie was paid in cash at the end of every shift. Before they started spending their earnings on frivolities, they needed to save enough money for the first three months' rent by late December. This was crucial for their plan to work. They did agree, however, that a new helmet that properly fit over Donnie's wavy black hair was a necessity worth spending money on.

Megan's sister, Kara, came home from college one week before Christmas. It was her first year away at school and Megan's mother had missed her a great deal. Megan missed her too but for selfish reasons. Without her big sister around, Megan's mother's doting was no longer spread between the two of them. Megan caught the full force of it. She loved her mom and she enjoyed the attention, but sometimes it got to be too much. Megan was also happy to see her big sister because Kara, unbeknownst to her, was a vital component in renting the storage unit.

The day after Christmas, Kara slept in just as she had done every day since she had returned home. Megan liked to sleep in, too, but on the twenty-sixth of December, she had to wake up early. On most days when her alarmed buzzed, she was reluctant to get out of bed. On the day following Christmas, she had no trouble springing out of it. Megan dressed in blue jeans and a pretty, new sweater that she had just unwrapped the day before.

Without windows on the east wall of the room, very little sunlight slipped through the closed shades of Kara's bedroom. Megan waited in the doorway to confirm the rhythmic breathing of her slumbering sister. Careful to test the floor for potential squeaks before putting the full weight of her body down with each step, Megan quietly moved toward the dresser on which Kara's purse rested.

Megan had thought about asking her older sister if she could borrow her license for an hour, but Kara would want to know why. Megan didn't want her to know because Kara could someday use it against her as blackmail. Megan also couldn't tell her because she had made a promise with Donnie not to tell anyone. So, she had to "borrow" it without Kara knowing that she was "lending" it.

When reaching inside Kara's purse for her wallet, Megan's fingers came across a couple of unfamiliar items. Megan seldom carried a purse and curiosity made her pull them out. The darkness of the room prevented her from fully figuring out what they were, but she had a few ideas. They were items that Kara shouldn't have or, at least, things that their parents would not approve of being in her purse.

This raised the stakes. If Kara awoke to find Megan snooping around in her purse, there would be trouble because Kara had secrets of her own that she would be forced to pro-tect. Megan quickly put those items back, pulled out Kara's wallet, ascertained which piece of plastic was her driver's license, removed it, and left the bedroom.

She needed to have that license back in Kara's purse before she woke up to avoid conflict which might jeopardize the storage-unit project. Her big sister would not be happy about her little sister impersonating her.

Megan Priddy darted out the front door and across the street to Donnie's house. It was the first time she had ever rang Donnie's doorbell.

When he answered, Megan peeked past him. Heavy drapes blocked out the morning sun. There weren't even Christmas lights illuminating the room. She glanced around. She didn't see a Christmas tree. The house was dark except for the glow of a television.

"I've got it," she told him. "We have to hurry."

"Right now?" Donnie hadn't been expecting Megan this early and the only reason he was up was because hunger drove him from his bedroom to the kitchen. "Are they open?"

"Yes! Remember? I called them last week."

"Oh, yeah."

It was apparent to Megan that Donnie didn't appreciate the urgency of their mission.

"Donnie!" Megan said sharply without raising her voice. "We've got to go right now!"

"All right. Let me grab my money and a jacket."

"Hurry."

He didn't offer for her to wait inside. He closed the door halfway and disappeared. It didn't take long for him to reappear in the doorway.

He called back, "Mom! Going out! Be back in a little!" He reached for the door with his right hand.

Megan's impatience was growing. She took hold of his left hand and urged, "Hurry!" With his right hand grasping the doorknob, she pulled on his opposite hand, forcing him toward her. This chain reaction caused Donnie to yank on the door until it slammed closed.

F I V E

To ensure that Donnie maintained the quick pace she desired, Megan didn't release his hand until they were down his sidewalk and off their street. She was anxious to complete their errand and return Kara's driver's license to its proper place before it was discovered missing. Megan didn't have time to think about holding Donnie's hand. She had grabbed it to get him moving just as she would have grabbed anybody's.

For Donnie, it was something new and unexpected. He knew that Megan's intention was nothing more than an effort to get him moving along, but that didn't prevent him from taking pleasure from it. There had been previous physical contact between them. Such as when it was someone else's turn on a video game, one would gently shove the other out of the way. Or if one of them made fun of the other, they would receive a playful smack on the arm.

Never before had their hands touched. This was a new sensation for Donnie. He had never realized how intimate two hands clasped together could be. Nearly everything humans did was with their hands. Everything from scooping ice cream to picking up golf balls to changing television channels to taking tests. There were a countless number of tasks that people performed with their hands. Megan used the very hand that Donnie was holding for all kinds of things, including brushing her groovalicious hair. He had never felt as close to Megan as he did when they briskly walked along hand in hand.

Eventually, Megan let go and passed the driver's license to Donnie.

"This is Kara?" Donnie asked. Megan had told him the plan and how it involved her.

"Think we look alike?" Megan was starting to feel somewhat tense. She never thought that she looked as much like her sister as everyone said she did.

"You have some similar features. Your eyes are better."

"Thanks. Would you believe that's me?"

"Your hair is totally different." Donnie had never seen hair like Megan's. It was uniquely colored – subdued, yet exciting and alluring. He knew that he couldn't be the only person who sometimes wondered what it would feel like to touch.

Megan knew that her greatest attribute was her hair. On days when she looked in the mirror and nothing else seemed to look right, she was always able to look at her hair and say, "Wow. That looks boffo." It was silky and plush and just brushed the tops of her shoulders when she walked.

Megan's mom had initially vetoed her request to have it professionally highlighted. Megan pleaded with her for days. She wanted a totally fresh look when she started at her new school. Mrs. Priddy gave in. She couldn't stand seeing Megan upset about something she had control over.

The hairstylist helped Megan choose a cut that worked for her, but she had the color predetermined. Megan's inspiration came from the official state fruit of her new home. Setting a peach on the counter in front of the hairstylist, she said, "I want all of these colors mixed together." It took three hours for the hairstylist to meticulously blend the various shades of red, orange, yellow, and a hint of white. The combination was gorgeous, unique, and dazzling.

"That's no big deal," she said to Donnie about the difference in hairstyles. "If they say anything about my hair, I'll just say that I got it done different since the picture was taken."

Donnie finished his inspection of the license and handed it back. "Well, it's not the best photo, so I think that you'll be able to pull it off."

He didn't accompany Megan past the street corner of the block where Parkside Storage was located. Donnie wished her luck, gave her his half of the money, and she went on without him. His eyes stayed with her until she vanished inside the storage center.

The brown and orange office was small and warm. The walls were covered with packing materials, box samples, and other retail items for sale. Behind the counter were a computer, printer, and other office materials.

Megan thought that she heard a toilet flush before a man with thinning blonde hair appeared from beyond the main office. According to the nametag, his name was Rex.

"Can I help you?" The employee's slight southern drawl was effeminate. At first glance, he appeared to be a tidy individual. Beneath it, Megan sensed an unkempt person. She immediately felt uncomfortable being alone with him.

She swallowed her apprehension and replied, "I'd like to rent a storage unit."

His voice was condescending, "What are *you* going to do with it?"

Megan managed to stutter a few sounds but nothing that came out would have passed for the English language.

"Oh, chillax," he told her, spreading his fingers wide. "I'm kidding. I don't care what you do with it. We're at half-capacity. I'm just happy to rent it to you." He began tapping the keys on the keyboard. "We offer units from thirty-five to four-hundred square feet. All units have drive-up access. None of them are climate controlled so if you have stuff that might melt, I'm going to have to refer you to one of our other facilities."

She briefly wondered how hot it might get in the summer before replying, "That's fine."

"What size did you have in mind?"

Megan already had this figured out. The previous night she had referred to the notes that she had taken when she first called Parkside Storage. "Two-hundred square feet," she said.

The man continued typing on his computer. "Our most popular size. It runs ten by twenty feet. Will that suit your needs?"

"Yes."

"And would you like to take advantage of our special?" Rex began a speech that he had given many times before, "If you sign a one-year lease and pay the first three months forthright, then your initial month only costs nine dollars. Each month thereafter costs one-hundred nineteen dollars. You're subjected to a mulct for early termination. Upon expiration of the original lease, it converts to month-to-month. Thereafter, you can cancel anytime without penalty."

Megan was aware of her tendency to pull back on her lower lip with her two incisors when processing unfamiliar information. She tried to refrain from doing this when Rex spoke about the lease. She was bright enough to figure out his jibber-jabber if she had the time. She considered asking questions for clarification but didn't want to arouse suspicion by inquiring for answers that were obvious to everyone but her.

She blurted, "K. That's good," even if it really wasn't.

Rex pulled out a clipboard with paperwork attached. "Just fill this out, and I'll need to see your driver's license."

Megan set her sister's license on the counter and began filling in the requested information on the forms. She was careful to fill in Kara's name. The page was covered with fine print detailing descriptions of rights and obligations that she failed to fully comprehend or even read all the way through. For a moment, she thought that maybe she was in over her head.

"This," Rex declared, "is an out-of-state license."

Megan mentally used a cuss word before audibly concurring.

Rex took in a deep breath and exhaled dramatically. "New to the area?" he said.

Beyond her control, Megan's hands started to sweat. The pen became slippery and her fingers began to stick to the paper.

"Yes." She tried to sound confident when she said it, but it came out all wrong. She sounded like a timid ten-year old.

Rex nodded and handed the license back. Megan didn't know if that was a good sign or not.

He said, "Can I give you some advice?"

Megan didn't trust her words to come out right so she nodded her head.

"Hurry up and get your Georgia license 'cause this picture doesn't do you justice, sugar."

Megan painfully giggled a "Thank you." She would have been flattered by the compliment since Rex was really saying that she was more attractive than her older sister, but she was too nervous to be excited.

"How will you be paying today?" he said.

"Cash."

Rex smiled, showing off exactly which teeth were missing. "We accept cash."

The total before tax was two-hundred sixty dollars and ninety-five cents. This also included the price of a lock. Rex began keying in her information from the clipboard. Knowing that he was typing in her home address and the fact that Kara could wake up any minute tormented Megan.

She had the cash ready and waiting for him. He wrote down the gate password and unit number on a Parkside Storage bi-fold card and exchanged that for the money.

"Now, you can either walk out the back with me," Rex said, "or if you want to drive your car, you can follow me on the golf cart to your unit."

Megan had what she wanted. She needed to get out of that office and back to the house so she could return the driver's license. "Not necessary," she told Rex. "I'm in a hurry. I'll just find it the next time I come."

She turned and made haste for the door.

"Wait!" Rex called to her.

Megan Priddy already had one hand on the door, ready to push it open. Something was wrong, she thought. She messed up. Rex caught her falsifying information. She put on her fake smile that everyone found adorable and turned to face the creepy man.

"Come here," he instructed her.

She thought about bolting out the door and down the street, forfeiting the money she gave him. She couldn't. Rex had all of her personal information. Well, he had a mixture of Megan's and Kara's personal information.

Without losing her smile, Megan took a few steps back toward the counter.

"You've got change coming," the man said and handed her a few bucks and coins. "You really are in a hurry, aren't you, sugar?"

"Yeah," Megan took the money and shoved it in her pocket. "Bye."

Donnie saw her reappear from the office. She was nearly running toward him. He thought they might be in trouble. She didn't stop once she got to him. All she said was, "Come on."

"What happened?"

Not breaking stride, she looked up at him. "We did it."

Nothing lit up Donnie's dark features like his smile. Unlike Megan, he didn't possess any fake expressions. Unless he was wearing a genuine smile, his face was solemn in every picture that was taken of him. Megan loved seeing that smile. It was a treat.

She stopped walking and admired it. It was infectious, and she smiled back.

"That's awesome," he told her. "I want to hear about it."

"I have to get home. If my sister finds out I swiped her license…," she didn't exactly know the end of the sentence. There were many potential outcomes. Some worse than others. Getting everything back to normal was the safest play.

"Which one did we get?"

Megan looked down at the Parkside Storage bi-fold card for the first time. "Unit #143."

S I X

Storage Unit #143 felt like a basement built above ground. Three of the walls were comprised of concrete block and the fourth wall was a metallic rolling garage door that lifted manually. The unit was lit by a single exposed light bulb that screwed into the ceiling at the center of the unit. Its switch was on the wall, near the door.

New Year's Day was the first time that Donnie and Megan tested out the storage unit. They didn't stay very long. The air was frigid and the cold of the cement floor froze their butts and traveled up their spines like mercury in a thermometer.

On the first day back to school after winter break, both of them went to the student store during lunch. The blankets left over from football season were on sale and Donnie and Megan each bought one, not out of school spirit for the Haviland High Platypuses, but out of necessity. They could sit on the blankets and wrap them around their bodies until the weather turned warm or until they came up with a better solution for the cold.

They didn't make it five steps out of the student store before Sada, the school's anti-everything girl and Megan's lunch-table companion, caught them with their purchases. Her hair was blacker than outer space and she had the make-up on to match. No matter the time of day, she always sounded sleepy when she spoke. "You've got to be kidding me," she said, offended that they would support anything that had to do with their school. "What are you guys doing with those?"

Megan told her, "Mine is a belated Christmas present for you."

"Riiiight. It will go great with my pom-poms and H.H.S. Platypuses sweatshirt. Hey! While you guys are here, can you sign my petition? I'm running for student council."

"You say that jokingly, Sada," Megan replied with a grin, "but I know deep down you hope to be Homecoming Queen someday."

"Sha-right. But if I were," she moved to within inches of Donnie, "I'd want you to be my king." She chomped her teeth together near his face and went back into the lunch room.

Donnie shook his head in wonder. "She's not even weird to get attention. She's just weird 'cause she is."

"Not really," Megan disagreed.

"No?"

"You just have to hang with her for a little to understand."

"The girl hates everything."

"Nah. She's open-minded."

"About as open minded as an aardvark."

Neither of them were model students that afternoon. They sat in their seats and looked at the teacher, but neither of them paid attention to the lesson. Donnie and Megan couldn't stop thinking about their new hangout. It was a private club for just the two of them. They couldn't wait to go.

Usually after school they moved at a snail's pace. The freedom from authority always felt good and they were never in a hurry to reach their next destination and resume their role as teenagers. The first day back to school after winter break was different. They had a place to go where they were the authorities.

They moved down Memory Lane so fast that the Richie's dog barely had time to get in two barks before the kids were past its fence.

Before blowing by Swifts, Donnie asked, "Wanna stop here for a couple of hot chocolates?"

"K, but let's not dilly-dally."

Donnie bought a large while Megan opted for a small. She declined marshmallows. He accepted her unused portion.

Donnie was halfway out the door when Megan exclaimed, "Look what they got!"

"What?" He reentered Swifts.

She pointed to bin of plush piglets next to the magazine rack. "I want one."

"What are you telling me for? Buy one."

"I mean, like a real one. I want a little pig. They're my favoritest. Look how cute they are."

"I don't think that a real pig would be quite as cute."

"Oh yeah, it would be. And those little ones, they make the cutest noises."

Megan kept staring at the bin of pigs. Donnie pulled his hat back on and buttoned his jacket while he waited for her to purchase one of the stuffed animals or make a move toward the door. Eventually, he said, "Are you gonna get one of those or what?"

Startled by his voice, she shook her head and said, "No."

"Let's go."

He pushed the door open and held it for her.

A block away was Parkside Storage. They walked up the driveway and entered their code on a keypad that rose from the ground. This activated a long gate, wide enough for customers to drive their cars through. It eased its way to the right.

Unit #143 was located at the far end of the first row. It faced west and another row of replica storage units.

With a rattle and clang, Donnie whipped open the unit. Megan flipped on the bare light and claimed the wall on the right side. Donnie pulled the door down and took the wall opposite her.

Both kids silently wrapped themselves in their newly purchased blankets and made themselves as comfortable as they could by sitting on a portion of the blanket and leaning against the wall.

She began digging through her satchel. He waited, curious to see what she was going to pull out. When it was a schoolbook and some paper, he asked, "What are you doing?"

Reaching for a purple pen from the side pocket of her satchel, she answered, "Homework."

"No joking?"

"For real." The book was open on her lap.

Donnie sipped his hot chocolate. "Boy, I could have saved us from getting jobs to pay for this place if I would've shown you where the Haviland library is."

Megan began copying a math problem from her book to paper. Without raising her head, she looked at Donnie with just her eyes. "I know where the library is, Donnie." Her gaze returned to her paper. "I just like to get my homework done first, is all. It won't take me long. I only have math today. I can do the reading for social studies in bed tonight." She knew that Donnie's grades could be better if he applied himself and suggested, "You might want to do the same."

"Read my social studies in your bed tonight?"

Megan looked up just long enough to give him her "ha-ha, very funny" look.

Donnie took his five-subject notebook from his backpack and began jotting down miscellaneous thoughts, none of which had anything to do with homework. Once he emptied his head of the day's contemplations, he took a book from his backpack and read.

Megan finished her math homework in half an hour. She looked across the unit at Donnie and the book that he was reading. "*Charlie and the Chocolate Factory*?"

Donnie looked up and asked, "What about it?"

"Isn't that a kid's book?"

Donnie slipped in a marker and closed the book. "It was when I got it, but now I suppose that it's a teen's book. You know, since I'm sixteen and all." He flipped the book over and admired the front cover. The jacket was crinkled along the edges and the ink was faded, but like a handsome man, it grew more distinguished with age. "I suppose if I still own it when I turn eighteen, it'll be an adult's book."

Donnie's semantic games annoyed her but not in a bad way. "What I meant was, wasn't that book written for children?"

"Do you assume that just because it has children in it?"

"I never read it."

"You should. It's my favorite book."

"I should read it because it's your favorite book?"

"You should read it because it's good. Charlie Bucket is a marvelous hero."

"What does he save?"

"You don't have to save stuff to be a hero."

Megan wanted to flip through the worn book but feared losing the warmth she had accumulated while sitting snug in her blanket so she stayed put and inquired from her spot, "How long have you had it?"

"Fifth grade. I try to keep it nice. It was a birthday gift from my father. He read one chapter a night to me. Thirty nights in all. It's the only book I can remember him ever reading to me."

Megan blew out and fluttered her lips. "That's one more than my dad's ever read to me." She took a pair of mittens that matched her knitted hat with a purple tassel out of her coat pockets. "Instead of reading that," she said, "why don't you read your assigned chapters for school?"

"I prefer fiction."

"Why?"

Donnie slid *Charlie and the Chocolate Factory* into his backpack. "I don't know. Maybe 'cause I like reading about imaginary things. Stuff that can't happen or would be really far out if it did. You know, fantasies that someone drew up because they don't already exist. What's so great about your school crap?"

"The opposite of your fiction. It's cool 'cause it's not made up. If you read this stuff and really think about it…"

"Yeah," he interrupted, "that's what I really want to spend my time thinking about."

She ignored him, "If you read it, I mean read it and take your time to absorb it, like take your time and imagine what was happening, it's some of the most screwed up stuff you'll read. And the really crazy part is that it's all true."

Donnie zipped his backpack closed. "Substitute the word 'boring' for 'true'."

"Whatever."

Donnie stood. "It's cold. You ready to go?"

Megan got her things together. "Yeah. We need a radio."

Donnie never listened to the radio, but it didn't sound like a bad idea.

SEVEN

Megan had homework nearly every day. On days that she had a lot, she walked ahead while Donnie stopped at Swifts to make their snack and beverage purchases. Later, when he arrived at Unit #143, Megan would be sitting against her wall with a blanket wrapped around her and textbooks surrounding her.

Stopping at Swifts for the snacks could not be considered a sacrifice for Donnie. He thoroughly enjoyed the Swifts's experience. Even though it was cold out, he always checked the flavors on the Polar Slurp machine, just in case they snuck in a new one. He enjoyed looking for new brands of candy and to see what knick knacks were currently stocked. If anyone was ever out of touch with what was happening in America, all they had to do was stop at Swifts to find the latest fad.

It was the first Monday in February when Donnie said, "I'll catch up with you at Unit #143. I'm gonna cross the street to Swifts and grab a couple hot chocolates and some snackage."

While he was checking for traffic, he heard her say, "Not so much fatty stuff from now on, K?" Megan said it with just enough concern in her voice for Donnie to know to take her seriously.

He turned slowly back around. "Swifts doesn't have a lot to offer in the way of nutrition."

"I know," she resigned, "but could you try?"

Donnie honestly did not know how to go about that and asked, "How?"

"You can start by making my drinks diet."

"I don't think the hot chocolate comes in diet."

"On the days you get hot cocoa, I'll take coffee with artificial sweetener."

"Coffee?" Donnie cupped his hands around his mouth, exhaled, rubbed them together, and then shoved them deep into his pockets. "What gives? You're worried about your weight?"

Megan wasn't TV sit-com thin like a lot of the girls who attended Haviland High, but she wasn't built for the wrestling team either.

"I've put on a few pounds since we started hanging out."

"I can't tell." He wasn't saying it just to be nice. Donnie really could not tell.

"I could and I got on the scale to check and there they were."

"What's a few pounds? You're still growing, you know?"

"I'm not built like you, Donnie. You're just like ultra-skinny with the metabolism of a sea otter."

"Sea otters have high metabolism?"

She waved her hand dismissively. "Yeah. I saw it on PBS last night."

"You watch PBS?"

"Donnie!"

"Sorry."

The tip of her nose was turning pink from the cold. Donnie found this attractive for reasons beyond his comprehension.

"I used to be… Well, I used to be… chunky… hefty," she confided.

"Really?" Since he only knew her to be this one size, her declaration took him by surprise.

"It's very important to my mom that I'm happy and for the first thirteen years of my life she was doing it with food. All that excess was adding the padding. A slice of 'za is no biggie, but she was feeding me half the pizza and following it with a plate of homemade chocolate cake. She doesn't work, you know, so she'd spend a good hour at the grocery store every day thinking up the things she could bake for me. Us, really. She's kind of fat." Megan cringed slightly at her own words. "Not really fat, but," she searched for a better synonym with which to describe her mother, "well, she's got a few extra pounds. It doesn't seem to bother her though, so..."

Donnie admired her forthrightness. Wasn't she scared that he would make fun of her?

"Twenty-seven pounds," she informed him. "That's how much I lost. I'm not like an anorexic or anything. I'll eat a Twinkie once a week, no prob, but it's best not to have a box, or even a twin pack, around 'cause sometimes it's hard for me to stop." She rubbed her nose with a purple mitten. "My mother is now forbidden to make Rice Krispie treats."

Donnie looked across the street and tried to recall the snack aisle's offering. "I'll do my best," he said. "I think they have some baked potato chips or something." He reached a hand under his hat and scratched the side of his head. "I've never really looked to see if they have low-fat stuff..." He shrugged his shoulders. The street was clear and he took off.

It was too easy for Megan Priddy to remember what it was like to be large. People treated her differently. It wasn't always intentional, but it happened. For example, Donnie, on that first day when she had asked him to walk home with her, may not have been interested in her offer. It wouldn't have been a conscious decision. The shape of her body would have sent a subliminal message warding him off. Or, he may have walked home with her that day but would have been sure to avoid her for the rest of the school year.

She entered the code for the gate and while she waited for it to open, changed her mind. Maybe that was how most people would have treated her, but not Donnie. He was too wholesome. His sight traveled past an individual's superficial features. Their friendship was based on who they were and not what they looked like.

Donnie wore a ski mask during the winter to keep the flesh on his face from freezing when he rode his bicycle. He always double-checked with his hand to make sure that the front mask portion was pulled up over his head and off his face before entering Swifts. He didn't want to catch a shotgun blast in the chest because he was mistaken for a robber.

He skipped his usual video game and headed straight to the storage unit after he bought one hot chocolate, one coffee, and a large bag of baked cheese puffs. He'd share the healthier puffs with her, but there was no way that he was doing the coffee.

He arrived at the storage unit fifteen minutes after Megan. She was already cozied up in her blanket and working away on her schoolwork. Donnie found her discipline attractive and usually made it a point not to interrupt her while she worked.

The reason he passed on video games was to prepare for an oral presentation due the next day. He may have slacked off when it came to studying but not when it involved standing alone, in front his peers. He extracted a stack of index cards bound by a rubber band from his backpack and began reviewing his notes.

Megan blurted, "I exercise."

She suddenly felt warm in the cold storage unit and removed her knitted hat that held her enchanting tresses pressed against her ears.

"We have a treadmill," she felt compelled to explain, "in our basement, that I use."

Now that Donnie knew her secret, she could not get it off her mind. When she looked at Donnie, she was certain that he was thinking of her as the fat girl she once was. He wasn't really. His mind was on improving his oral presentation, but hers was obsessing on her previous appearance. Someone now knew. She had escaped her past only to drag it up again.

Megan rambled like the teenage girl she was, "It's really my dad's. He works like all day long. Then he comes home and runs on that thing while he watches some business news money crap on TV. We don't even have dinner together half the nights. My mom makes him take her out every Saturday. If she didn't, she'd never see him..."

Donnie realized that Megan was freaking. His tender voice was like a massage for the ears, "I don't care that you were fat, Megan."

His sincere acceptance of her caught Megan off-guard and she nearly divulged the true color of her hair. She was glad to have found someone at her new school that she could open up to but was surprised that it was a boy. She felt safe with him. Donnie was someone she could tell anything, but she held back on revealing too much about her hair. A girl's got to have some secrets.

Donnie shuffled a few of his cards around and Megan chewed her pen cap. Their concentration was broken and they were thinking about things other than their homework.

Donnie asked, "Why do you suppose your mom tries so hard to make you happy?"

Megan took the pen out of her mouth and placed the tip against the paper even though she didn't have anything to write. "I think because she's not."

They didn't speak after that and eventually their minds went back to their schoolwork.

Using the note cards that contained the keywords for his presentation in neat block letters, Donnie practiced his four-minute speech several times in his head.

When Megan was changing subjects and putting one book away while getting another out, she noticed him silently mouthing the words and asked, "Are you practicing your oral presentation?" Even though she had a different teacher, they were doing oral presentations in her English class as well.

"Yeah."

"Why don't you practice it once in front of me?"

"Nah." He shook his head. "I don't think so."

"C'mon, you're going to do it in front of everyone and you can't do it in front of me? If you show me yours, I'll show you mine."

Donnie considered this. Practicing out loud would have its benefits. "All right. Let's do it."

"K. You first."

Megan Priddy honestly believed that practicing would help Donnie prepare, but she also wanted to see him perform. She wanted the opportunity to dissect every word he pronounced. She wanted to stare at his wavy black-haired head, his pudgy cheeks, and his elongated body without feeling funny about it. She wanted to admire Donnie Betts.

Donnie moved to the back wall and launched into his oral presentation. It felt strange performing for just one person, but he practiced it just as if there were twenty-five.

She was stunned by the professionalism of his presentation. It was as if Donnie became another person. His shy persona was devoured by the charismatic kid that she, until now, had only seen glimpses of. He was informative and entertaining. She could have easily watched him for an hour. Anyone could have.

Megan also learned a few things about Donnie that weren't mentioned in his speech. Underneath his awkward charm, there was an undefined bubble of potential waiting to escape. For the first time, Megan saw it. It was mesmerizing.

When Donnie finished, he had to ask, "Well? How is it?"

The words crept from her mouth, "It was un-freaking-believable."

EIGHT

Things were slow at work during January and February. The inclement weather brought with it fewer shifts for each of them. Not many golfers wanted to practice their swing through several layers of clothing and the warm meals available at Friendly's were good, but the main reason people frequented the restaurant was for the cold desserts.

This provided Donnie and Megan with more time to spend at the storage unit but less money. It was important that they always pay a few months in advance to keep the Parkside Storage bills from being mailed to Megan's home. At least they would be in Kara's name if they were.

While some of their friends participated in after-school activities such as sports or clubs, Donnie and Megan's extracurricular activity was Unit #143. Their daily stop became a comfortable routine. Even on the days that they had to work, they would still stop in to unwind before heading off to start their shifts.

Donnie always finished his homework first, or more accurately, stopped first. He never rushed Megan to finish or encouraged her to quit. He'd end up reading a book or scribbling sentences of nonsense in his notebook. There weren't many notes in it so he had to fill it with something.

Some days, they would talk a lot. On others, like when Megan had plenty of homework, they would hardly speak at all. They didn't give it any thought. They didn't have to converse to enjoy each other's company. Simply existing together was oftentimes enough.

Fridays were their favorite. The school week was over and it was the only weekday that Megan didn't do her homework at the storage unit.

Donnie tossed his empty hot chocolate cup on the pile that had been accumulating for the past few weeks.

Megan glanced up from the school newspaper that she was reading to say, "We need a trash bag."

"And furniture."

"I won't argue that." Both were getting tired of their sparse storage unit. "How would we get it here?"

A few days earlier, Donnie had biked to the nearby store. He had done it many times in the past but never for something as big or heavy as a boom box. Even the required D batteries weighed him down. The combination radio, cassette, and CD player wouldn't fit in his backpack until he removed it from its cardboard packaging.

They usually listened to one of two stations. One exclusively played alternative rock and the other played a mixture of new and classic rock. Donnie found the music somewhat distracting to his reading and writing, but Megan was immune to it. He could manage to do math problems with it on in the background, but if he had to do any schoolwork that involved words, the lyrics of the song always seemed to interfere. He was conditioning himself to tune out the radio while he read, which made him wonder what the point was of having the radio on in the first place.

He didn't mind the distraction that occurred with some songs. He'd just stop and listen to it for a while. He not only listened to the words, but he carefully listened for the individual instruments and how they worked together.

Donnie answered Megan's question, "I definitely can't fit anything bigger than that boom box in my backpack."

"Are you going to have your license soon?"

"Not if I can't get someone to take me driving."

Megan set the newspaper aside and stretched her legs without standing. "Why don't your parents let you drive to the store and stuff so you can get the practice?"

"Because if I don't get the practice then I won't pass the test and if I don't pass the test they don't have to worry about me taking the car."

"You should tell them that it's too cold for you to bike to work."

"Even on the days I get a ride, my mom never lets me drive."

"What about your dad?"

"He doesn't take me to work."

When the DJ finally stopped yapping and played music, Megan jumped up and spun her way toward the radio. "This song is boffo groovalicious," she said while shimmying about to the tune with her blanket still wrapped around her.

"It's good."

The verses were meager, but the chorus was catchy.

"Doesn't it make you want to dance?" she said, smiling.

"I've never had a song make me want to dance."

"But you do dance, right?"

No. Donnie Betts was not a dancer. He was built long and skinny and without the chip required for physical coordination. Donnie hoped that it was still under development and someday would be installed in his brain. All Megan seemed to be doing was shuffling her feet from side to side, so he said that he did dance and joined her.

Halfway through the song, Megan let her blanket drop and grabbed Donnie by the arms. "What about Sada?" she said. "Sada has her license. She'll take us to the store for what we need."

"She'll ask questions."

"Maybe she will. Maybe she won't."

"We can't take that chance. Plus, we can't bring her to the storage unit anyway."

"That's true."

Both of them stopped dancing while they worked it out. In ten minutes, they came up with a feasible plan for scoring some necessities for Unit #143.

After checking out several different lunch tables when she first started attending Haviland High, Megan decided to eat regularly at Sada's table. It was a hodgepodge of voluntary outcasts from various cliques. One girl was a jock who played whatever sport was in season and another was into journalism. There was a cheerleader, a punkster, the class treasurer, and the girl who consistently set the curve on Algebra exams. Megan's role, of course, was the new girl.

Sada may have been the prettiest girl in school, but it was difficult to tell under her heavy mascara, dark cherry lipstick, and hair dyed so black that it sometimes shined a deep blue. If someone were to like Sada, they were forced to like her for who she was and not what she looked like. This rarely happened at Haviland High. Despite her shoddy clothing, Sada lived in an affluent neighborhood and drove an SUV to school every day.

After lunch on Wednesday, Megan approached Sada with her request.

The story was that Megan was going to have a surprise anniversary party for her parents for which she needed a card table and two chairs. Since it was a surprise, Donnie would have to accompany them and the goods would have to be stored at his house until it was time for the party.

Megan did not like concocting this lie for Sada, but her

loyalty was with Donnie and the secrecy of the storage unit.

It was a flimsy story. Why a card table and why only two chairs? Megan prepared a yarn about their first date at her father's apartment when he was poor and could only afford a card table with two chairs. She'd use this extension of the lie only as a last resort.

Scheduling was tricky. They would have to drop the stuff off while Donnie's house was vacant so he could stash the goods where they wouldn't be found. Megan's house would have been available Saturday night, but Sada was not. Plus, Megan's mom was into everything and would have found the purchased supplies if they were in the house. How would Megan explain that?

It was set for Friday night. Sada would pick them up around six and they would go to the mall. Before the night was over, they would make the necessary purchases and drop the stuff off at Donnie's house.

The two girls stopped at Megan's locker before class.

"What's he like?" Sada sounded groggy, like she was just napping instead of eating lunch.

"Who? Donnie?" Megan asked. "You've known him longer than I have."

"Everyone in this school has."

"So you should be telling me."

"You'd think."

Megan pushed her locker shut. "He's nice. He's easy to talk to."

"Are you kidding?"

"No. Why? What's your impression of him?"

"We used to call him glass of milk," Sada told her. "You know? Wholesome. Like a glass of milk. Kind of innocent. For a while I even thought that he was datable, but he's such a good kid. I didn't wanna corrupt him."

"Maybe some of his good traits would have rubbed off on you."

"Yeah, well, either way…"

They entered the classroom but avoided the other students. The late bell had yet to ring.

"If things go cool Friday, maybe we'll see a movie next week," Sada said.

Megan's one word reply, "Yeah," came out slowly. She was trying to figure out if Sada meant the three of them, the two of them, or Sada and Donnie.

Speaking even softer now, Sada said, "I just never know how to treat him."

Megan laughed at this. "What are you talking about?"

"Since the thing with his dad came out, he's kept to himself. I really don't know what to say…"

"What about his dad?"

"You don't know?"

"Know what?"

The late bell rang and they took their seats. Megan didn't hear a word the teacher said for the entire period.

As soon as the bell rang, she jumped from her seat and asked Sada, "What about Donnie's father?"

NINE

Three or four times a month, Megan stayed after school an extra fifteen minutes to meet with a teacher for a little extra help with her homework. Donnie would walk ahead and purchase their drinks or snacks from Swifts and then go on to the storage facility and wait for her. She sometimes caught up to him if he became absorbed in a video game.

On March 8th, Donnie was the one to stay after school. At least, that's what he told Megan.

He was disappointed that he received a B instead of an A on his oral presentation. Donnie scored A's on occasion, but it wasn't a common grade for him. He did know that he deserved an A for his presentation and he was determined to get it.

It was an easy presentation for him. The topic was jobs and he talked about working at Dirt's driving range. He especially felt comfortable with his topic because no one could dispute his information since no one else worked for Dirt. His public-speaking skills came naturally and instinctively. Donnie was born with what actors called "presence." When he was in front of a crowd, it was difficult for others to look away. They felt compelled to watch him.

When Mr. Colby asked for volunteers to go first, Donnie Betts was the only student to raise his hand. This caught a few of the students' attention and it definitely caught the teacher's. Donnie seldom raised his hand in any of his classes. He wasn't adverse to it; he just never cared to interact with the class. He preferred the role of silent observer.

In a perverse way, Donnie actually looked forward to going first. He wanted to set the bar high for everyone else. He wanted his presentation to be so fascinating that the other students were even more intimidated; thus, making his presentation look even better.

Mr. Colby was renowned for giving very few A's for oral presentations. Certainly some students had to score A's, though. Donnie saw no reason for him not to be one of those students.

Megan, who had a different teacher, but whose class was following the same curriculum, dreaded giving her oral presentation. She was a cute, charismatic, and gifted girl. She had nothing to fear, yet she was horrified of standing in front of her classmates. Donnie thought this through one day in Unit #143 while he was writing down a few notes for his speech. Everyone would be so self-conscious and focused on their performance that it wouldn't take much to do something stellar.

When the day came and he finally stepped in front of his class, Donnie felt the proverbial butterflies. For a moment, just a moment, he became nervous. Then he reminded himself that everyone, if they admitted it or not, would suffer from the anxiety of being in front of their classmates. Donnie was in control. He smiled at this thought and that smile set the tone for his speech.

He took those butterflies and put them to work. He harnessed the power of their fluttering wings and injected his speech with energy and an edge. He made eye contact with every student, at least the ones who actually were looking at him, and he saw that they were actively listening. They were interested. And they weren't only interested because his topic was cool, but because he captivated them with his commitment to the presentation. For a boy who didn't speak much,

Donnie had an incredible amount of confidence speaking in front of a classroom with twenty-five students.

In his opening, Donnie rhetorically asked, "How would you like to be paid for having golf balls launched at you?" He went on to clarify that really wasn't his job, but on some days it felt like it. Donnie said that he enjoyed working outdoors even when the weather wasn't ideal. It was similar to picking up litter but more dignified. He often set his own hours, but was responsible for ensuring that the shack never ran out of golf balls to sell.

He concluded by telling his two stories about being hit. Neither time did he sustain a serious injury. Then, because he knew there were wise guys who would give it a try, he dared all of them to come out and take a whack at him. "If you think you can swing a metal club into a small white ball, hit it over one-hundred yards, and make contact with a moving target, then come and try it. Buckets are five bucks a piece and we'll take every cent you've got."

Mr. Colby only saw fit to give him a high B for his work. Donnie saw right through this. He knew that Mr. Colby was notorious for grading even tougher on the first of three consecutive oral presentations because he wanted to force his students to improve. Donnie wasn't about to let this happen to him. When the bell rang for lunch, Donnie held Mr. Colby at his desk and pleaded his case over and over. When Mr. Colby couldn't give ample enough reasons to justify the B, he was forced to grade Donnie's presentation on its merits. He changed the grade to an A.

"Donnie," Mr. Colby said right before Donnie left the room. Donnie reluctantly turned around.

The teacher set his glasses on his desk and leaned back in his chair, which reclined with the weight of his body. He said, "You could be president someday."

Donnie responded by leaving the room and going to lunch.

Since he had already taken care of his oral presentation grade during school, he didn't have to wait around afterwards to speak with his teacher. He had everything with him when the final bell rang so he could head straight for the storage unit without stopping at his locker. He needed to get there at least ten minutes before Megan.

It was her sixteenth birthday and he had plans to decorate Unit #143. He hung purple streamers around the top of the unit and blew up balloons as fast as he could without passing out.

He didn't know what to get her as a gift so he purchased, and wrapped the best he could, a few small gifts. Donnie got her three different types of purple pens, her favorite for doing homework or anything else that involved writing. He also got her a little stand to lean books on. She wouldn't be able to use it until they got the card table, but it would come in handy once they did. The last item was purchased at a second-hand store. It was a bracelet. He had the money to purchase a new one, but he didn't see any that fit her personality like the one at the consignment shop.

When he finished the decorations, he had leftover time to think about his gifts. Maybe he shouldn't have gotten her anything. Megan might get the wrong impression. Would she have done anything special for his birthday? None of that mattered, he thought. He wanted to decorate the storage unit and give her a few gifts because... well, because... because he liked her... as a friend... he cared for her. It was with Megan that he shared the storage unit, not anyone else. It was their secret. Their special secret. Just like their relationship was special.

The garage door shot up and banged to a stop when it reached the top.

"Donnie Betts!" Megan's hair twisted and writhed in the air like the snakes of Medusa. "You have some explaining to do!"

T E N

"**S**urprise?" he said.

Her mood momentarily lightened as she took in the streamers and balloons. Donnie could tell that she appreciated the mini-celebration he had put together for her. Then her eyebrows slanted down and in as she dropped her satchel against a side wall of the unit.

She met Donnie underneath the light. Her hands went to her hips. "You've been lying to me."

Donnie didn't understand. Was she upset with the lie about staying after school to get his grade fixed? That's ridiculous. He did it for her. It had to be something else, but he didn't know what.

"I feel like a fool," she went on. "You know, I thought you were all right."

"Huh?"

"I've been telling you everything. Private stuff that no one here knows! I trusted you." She crossed her arms.

"I haven't told anyone anything." It was the truth.

"No. It's what you've been keeping from me! Why didn't you tell me your dad…," then she couldn't say it. It was all she could think about since Sada filled her in, but now with Donnie, dear Donnie, standing right in front of her, she had to alter her words. Her voice softened some, "Why did you let me believe that your dad was still alive?"

Donnie Betts vanished. One second he was there. Then he was gone. His body remained behind, but it was only a vacant shell. He stood erect but motionless. His eyes were open but nothing that passed in their field of view registered in his mind. The central cog of his brain continued to rotate, but the other wheels didn't spin with it.

Megan suddenly felt alone in the storage unit. She became frightened. "Donnie?" Her voice became gentler. "Why didn't you tell me?"

She remembered when she had seen a similar look on him. It was on her first day of work at Friendly's. What was it that she said that day that made him quasi-comatose? Did she repeat those same words? No. That was something about finding a job. She hated seeing him in this state. She came to the miserable realization that she had overreacted and had been too harsh.

"I'm sorry, Donnie," she whispered. "I didn't mean to be so…" She wasn't getting through to him. He was gone. He was floating through a distant world. The only way for Megan to reach him was to purchase a ticket and join him there. "Donnie…" She took his hand in hers.

His lips barely moved, "Who told you?"

"Sada." Megan closed the distance between them. "Listen Donnie, I didn't mean to be so mean about it. I thought we could share whatever, you know? Like everything was safe in here. Everything between us. I thought we had an understanding. Why didn't you tell me?"

Donnie lightly rubbed a thumb against his lower lip. "How do you tell someone that?"

"Donnie, I'm your friend. I wouldn't hurt you. Why would you keep that from me? Why would you let me believe…?"

Donnie closed his eyes. "It's that everyone else knows. Everyone knows. It was nice to have someone who didn't." He took a breath and opened his eyes. "After he killed himself, I knew that nothing would ever be the same. That was that. My life and the world around me changed forever. But with you… with you, it was different. With you things were like they used to be. Like they were before people would see me and say, 'There's the kid whose dad committed suicide.'"

Megan Priddy hadn't thought it through from Donnie's perspective. "I'm sorry, Donnie. I didn't even think how much you must hurt. I did, some, but..."

Megan went from feeling like a fool because she was sharing her secrets with Donnie without his reciprocation to feeling like a fool because she had forgotten what it was like to escape a past where people try to pigeonhole you. Megan's own selfishness disgusted her.

To get his attention, she tugged on the sleeve of his hoodie and said, "Hey." Her glistening green eyes locked with his rich gray irises. "What I like is that you are who, who you are. That's what I dig about you. You don't try to impress me or be someone that you're not. And even the ones who say they don't care what others think, like Sada, really do. No matter how hard they try, they can't help caring at least just a little. You're the only person I've come across who truly doesn't. You're Donnie Betts and that's who I like hanging out with."

Donnie shivered from the cold.

"Come on," Megan said. "We'll share our blankets."

She folded hers over a few times and set it on the floor to keep their butts from freezing. Donnie joined her and they sat down together with the other blanket wrapped around them.

The story of his father's death was one that Donnie never told. It would require him to spontaneously speak more words than he had since the man's suicide.

"His problems started when he was laid off. Not his fault. They closed the local office. He was out of a job, along with one or two hundred others. It was announced a couple months before it happened so he started looking for another job right away. He tried. At first, he tried."

Donnie continued, the words echoing funny in his head and sounding foreign to his own ears. "With each unemployment check that arrived in the mail, he drank a little more. And the more he drank, the more depressed he got. That stuff you learn in eighth grade health class, you know, alcohol is a depressant, that's the truth. I've seen it. It would help him take one step forward before shoving him back two.

"But I didn't know how bad it was for a while. Everyone feels down from time to time, right? He was out of work for a few months. There's nothing unusual about feeling upset about that.

"We no longer could afford to go to the movies, but that didn't stop us from renting them. But, after a while, he stopped watching them with me. He'd say something about job searching and disappear. Or he'd halfway fall asleep while we were watching them. Then in the middle of the night, I'd hear the TV on. He'd complain about being tired, but he never seemed to sleep through the night.

"His drinking became noticeably worse and finding another job became a hopeless endeavor. He went through the motions, but it wasn't happening. 'Go find a job,' my mom would nag. Those words... 'Go find a job.' Like that would solve all the Betts's problems.

"One Saturday, we got fast food for dinner, just me and him. He hadn't eaten all day so I thought he'd order one of everything. All he got was one small chocolate milkshake. That was it.

"On the way back, he says, 'I'm sorry I let you down.' And his eyes got all puffy. I remember thinking, what's up? I didn't even know that he had let me down. How? You know? Why? What's he talking about? Are we broke? Do we have to sell the house? I didn't understand. I didn't understand, but I should have told him that I didn't feel let down at all. There were a few cutbacks we had to make, but him not having a job really didn't affect me.

"The next day, the school counselor pulled me out of class. She said that my mom was on her way to pick me up. When I asked her why, she told me about a car, a garage, carbon monoxide, and my dad. That's when I felt let down. It was the biggest letdown you can feel. And it's one that doesn't go away."

Although it was Donnie who had done all the talking, Megan was the one who felt breathless.

She looked around Unit #143 and saw the decorations and effort that Donnie had put into making her sixteenth birthday special. She spied a few gifts wrapped in shiny paper poking through his backpack. She placed a hand on her forehead. The words dripped from her mouth, "I am a total ass. I shouldn't have been so mad about it. You should have smacked me across the face." The thought never entered his mind. "It was hard for me to find out that you've been carrying this with you. To suddenly know that you've been alone with that when we spend so much time together. When we know so much about each other." She took a breath. "But, you're right. I didn't have to know." She took Donnie's hand and interlocked fingers with him, "Isn't it nice that I do, though?"

His head made a nearly imperceptible nod.

Their breathing was in sync. Their inhalations and exhalations worked together.

"You feel it, don't you?" she whispered.

"I do."

"What is it?"

"I don't know. Do you?"

She shook her head, causing her hair to drift in the air for a second before landing on her shoulders.

Megan wrapped her arms around him. It was the first time Donnie had been embraced since the funeral and he soaked it up. Megan unsuccessfully fought back tears.

"I'm sorry about your dad," she told him.

If her ear wasn't only a few inches away, she wouldn't have heard him say, "Happy birthday."

ELEVEN

Donnie watched out the front window of his house for Sada's SUV to pull into Megan's driveway. His mother was upstairs, getting ready for work. She worked four twelve-hour night shifts a week at a car manufacturing plant. It wasn't her ideal job, but she had to take it after his father's death in order to make ends meet.

He sat with his stocking feet on the couch and a book settled on his legs. His shoes and coat were nearby. Like a Revolutionary War minuteman, Donnie was ready to go at a moment's notice.

His mother entered the room, hair half done, makeup half applied. She was shorter than her only child. "Where are you going?" she asked.

"To the mall."

"With the girl across the street?"

"Megan. Yes. Sada from school is picking us up."

"I'll be at work when you get home." She abbreviated the three words "did you eat" into one by asking, "Jeet?"

"No."

She walked to the kitchen for her battered brown leather purse. "I'll give you five dollars for something at that food court. Tomorrow morning you can have cereal for breakfast. What time are you going to work?"

"Noon."

"I'll be here to take you. If I'm sleeping, wake me up. It's too cold to ride your bike."

"If I wake you up to take me, can I drive?"

His request was met with a gaze of disapproval. She handed him a five-dollar bill.

"Please, Mom," Donnie said without whining. "I want to get my driver's license."

Her son turned sixteen five months ago. She knew that she couldn't keep him off the roadways forever, but it seemed too soon.

Donnie pleaded his case by mentioning the attributes of having a driver's license. "I'll be able to run to the store when we need something. You wouldn't have to drop me off and pick me up if I go to the movies or something like that. I don't want to drive to school. I like walking. For most everything else, I ride my bike..."

"We only have the one car, Donnie," his mother interrupted.

"I just don't want to be trapped."

"What do you mean 'trapped'?"

"Like this," he said, pointing across the street. "If I want to go to the mall, I have to wait for someone else to go. I want to be able to leave the house and go places if I want to."

"Oh, Donnie…"

"I have to start driving sometime."

"You're not ready."

"Mom," Donnie took his eyes from his mother and put them on his book, "I think it's you who's not ready. And that's not fair."

She exhaled in defeat. Her son had always been independent, even before her husband's death. He was a good, responsible kid that she couldn't keep from growing up any longer. "OK. I promise to take you driving more often. We'll get your license. But don't expect the car anytime you want it."

"That's fine."

"And you have to promise me, *promise*, that you'll be careful every second that you are behind the wheel."

"Promise."

Sada's silver SUV pulled into Megan's driveway. The horn sounded. Donnie slipped on his shoes and shoved his arms through his coat sleeves. "Gotta go." They didn't hug or kiss good-bye, but before he left the house, he turned and said, "Thanks, mom."

Donnie and Megan piled in. Sada put the car in reverse but a tapping on the rear window kept her from lifting her foot off the break. Megan's mom was looking in at Donnie.

"Should I just go?" Sada asked Megan.

"I wish."

Donnie powered down the window to see what she wanted.

"Hi, Donnie." Her voice was full of cheer.

"Hey, Mrs. Priddy."

"What's your mother's name?"

"Betty."

"Is she busy tonight, do you know?"

"Yeah, she's going to work soon."

"Oh shoot! I was hoping that we could get together for a drink. Maybe another time?" She looked toward the front seat. "You kids have fun tonight. Not too late, Megan."

"All right, mom," she said. Her words confirmed that she wouldn't be late, but her tone carried a slight annoyance that let her mother know that she was delaying their departure.

Donnie closed his window and they pulled out of the driveway.

"Your mom is a chipper one," Sada said.

"Yeah." But she didn't mean it. Megan knew that it wouldn't last. After she was inside, alone with the door closed, her smile and energy would dissipate until either her daughter or spouse returned home.

Fifteen minutes later, Sada was parking the car at the Crosswynds Mall. They roamed around, checking out the latest fashions, music, and other mall goers.

While Megan and Sada investigated a sale on shoes, Donnie walked across the way to a musical instrument store. He wondered what Megan would think if he got a drum kit for the storage unit. He decided on a tambourine instead.

While they ate at the food court, Sada said, "You need a hat, Donnie B."

"What do you mean?"

"A baseball hat would be a solid investment for you."

Megan tried picturing him in one. "Yeah, you might want try it out."

"I have a hat," he said.

"Your ski mask?" Megan asked. "A baseball hat might be better for the days you're not on your bike."

"I totally dig that you're the only kid in school who dons a ski mask," Sada added, "but in another month it's going to be too hot."

He was fond of his ski mask. It kept his head and his face warm. Still, Megan and Sada seemed somewhat determined to find a baseball hat for him. So after they finished their meals, they walked to tHAT's tHAT.

The store was the size of a walk-in closet, but it was all hats. From floor to ceiling, hats were everywhere. The only areas not covered by hats were two small mirrors in the center of each wall on either side.

Donnie tried on a random hat and looked at himself in the mirror. The girls were right. It was a fashionable look for him. He noticed them in the mirror. They were each peeking over a shoulder at his reflection.

Megan was standing on her toes and couldn't see well. She instructed him to turn around. The girls took a few steps back and when he turned around, grins of accomplishment spread across their faces.

"Definitely," was Sada's one word of approval.

"Boffo," was Megan's.

"Really?" Donnie thought so too, but he wanted to make sure that they weren't putting him on. He looked at Megan, "A baseball hat?"

She nodded. She wanted to say more but refrained. She was embarrassed to tell him in front of Sada that the little ringlets of black hair escaping from the sides and back were very appealing.

He removed the hat from his head and put it back on the rack. "OK, yeah. Help me pick out a cool one."

"What about that one with a pirate on it," Sada said, pointing to the wall.

"A pirate?" Megan said. "I wonder what that's about?"

Donnie had to reach high for the goldenrod colored cap. "It's the Pittsburgh Pirates."

"Who?" the girls said in unison.

"The Pittsburgh Pirates. The baseball team."

Sada shook her head.

Megan shrugged her shoulders, "Never heard of them."

Sada asked a very reasonable question, "What are pirates doing in Pittsburgh?"

"You think that's weird?" Donnie said. "There's Penguins there, too."

He was about to try it on when Sada said, "Wait. Gimme," and swiped it from his hands.

The black bill of the cap was very flat and stiff. Sada took a minute to cup it in her hands, bending it and curving it. "I have an older brother," she explained. "You gotta shape the bill." She handed it back to Donnie.

Using both hands, he slipped it on over his mop. Something about the hat's colors made the little bit of black hair that showed shine and his gray eyes pop.

Sada put her thumb and index finger together in the universal sign for OK.

Megan adored him in it and she told him so.

He bought the hat.

T W E L V E

At 2:30 in the morning, Megan drifted in and out of consciousness to the sound of low volume rock music mixed with static. She rolled over and pulled her blankets tighter. The light sound of guitar, drums, and fuzz continued. Her eyelids lifted halfway. Everything was blurred as her eyes struggled to wake up enough to focus.

Her clock/radio read 2:32. The music she heard was her alarm. It was time for their planned late-night escapade.

She had to sneak out and meet Donnie so they could carry their furniture to Unit #143.

She remembered being at the mall with Donnie and Sada just a few hours earlier. When they left, it had taken Sada longer to open her newly purchased CD and insert it in the vehicle's player than it had for her to drive across the street to the discount retailer.

There, Donnie and Megan found a five-piece set for fifty dollars that included a card table and four folding chairs. They didn't need the extra two chairs, but everything came together in one package. Keeping with the charade that it was a surprise anniversary gift for her parents, Megan was the one who purchased it. She'd even up with Donnie later on.

Donnie thought the bare incandescent light bulb of the storage unit was too harsh. While they were at the store, he found a small lamp shade that he could affix upside-down to the light. To compensate for the dimmer illumination, he picked up an assortment of candles. He thought that Sada might question his odd purchases, but on the contrary, they seemed reasonable to her.

When they returned from their shopping spree, Sada backed into Donnie's driveway. He quickly unloaded the stuff from the back of the SUV and put it in his garage. He didn't have to worry about hiding it from his mother because they would take it to the storage unit before she came home from work the next morning.

Megan clicked her alarm off, yawned, and lay quietly for a few moments to make sure that she didn't hear anyone else roaming about. She maneuvered around in the darkness of her bedroom. Without removing her red flannel PJs, she pulled on a baggy pair of jeans, a bulky sweatshirt, and her purple tassel hat.

With the stealth of a cat closing in on its prey, Megan crept down the hall and past her parent's bedroom. She moved as quickly as she could without making sound. The center section of the staircase creaked from excessive use. She avoided it by carefully hugging the right edge of the steps.

Not counting the windows, there were three ways out of the Priddy's house: front door, back door, and garage door. The garage door would make a racket, so that escape route was immediately ruled out. She hesitated momentarily at the bottom of the stairs. Without making a conscious decision, her body turned left toward the back door. Before closing it behind her, she double-checked that it remained unlocked.

She came around the front of her house and headed directly to Donnie's. Her head swiveled left to right, scanning for any signs of life. She skittered across the empty street and onto Donnie's driveway. The night was calm and so was she until…

"Pssst!"

The sound was like an electric shock causing her to leap high enough to dunk a basketball.

"Over here," said a male's voice.

She looked toward the shadow between the two houses. Donnie stepped out so she could see him and then resumed his spot in the darkness.

Megan walked over and slapped him on the chest. "You scared me!" she said in a forceful whisper.

"How? You knew you were meeting me."

"But I didn't see you."

"Sorry."

It was on the chilly side and Donnie traded in his new Pirates cap for the ski mask.

Megan noticed the large square box leaning against the side of the garage. "Boy," she said, "that's really big. How are we going to get it there?"

"Carry it."

She tilted her head back, looked at the night sky, and then lowered it back down to face him. "I know we're going to carry it, Donnie. How are we going to get there without anyone seeing us?"

"It's like three o'clock in the morning. Who's going to see us?"

"Insomniacs."

"We'll keep off Memory Lane as much as we can and we'll move as fast as we can."

"We're going to get caught," Megan said hopelessly.

"By who?"

"The police? Isn't there a curfew?"

Donnie shrugged, "Probably."

Megan shrugged her shoulders and mimicked his lazy cadence, "Probably."

"I'll take the front. You get the back. I'll lead. Come on."

With the winter moon lighting their way, they headed off down the vacant side streets. This route was longer than taking the main street, but it was safer because of the minimal amount of traffic.

Halfway there, Megan said, "This is getting heavy."

"I'm sure that it weighs the same as when we left."

"You know what I mean."

Then, a few houses down and on the opposite side of the street, a garage door began to creak open and light spilled on to the driveway. While Donnie was trying to figure out where those people were going at three o'clock in the morning, Megan said, "Lay it flat on the sidewalk. Quick!"

As soon they had it down, both of them darted off to the first hiding spot they saw. Donnie went left into someone's front yard and hid behind a bush. Megan dashed into the nearby shallow woods of one of the few undeveloped lots.

They watched as the old car with chrome bumpers slowly backed out of the driveway. Their hope was that it would drive in the opposite direction. It didn't. A moment later, its headlights brightened the road directly ahead of Donnie. He held his breath as the vehicle approached. Even though they had laid the box flat, it still rose a good six inches off the ground. Donnie tried convincing himself that the people in the car would either be focused on the road and not see the box or see it and not be interested in it.

Although there was no sound reason behind it, his brain wanted to believe that the people in the car left their home with the sole purpose of spoiling their plans.

The car sped past without the slightest bit of hesitation and the crisis was over. Relief came, his breath returned, and his tense muscles relaxed.

After the car rounded the corner at the stop sign, Donnie reappeared and waited for Megan to come out of her hiding spot. Five seconds without seeing her was long enough to make him go looking.

He walked along the edge of the street near the woods, whispering her name. Finally, he heard, "Over here."

It took a second for his eyes to adjust to the darkness of the woods, but he found Megan. From her waist down, she dangled over an edge. The upper portion of her body clung to the ground.

"Donnie. Help." Despite the slight panic that she felt, her voice remained calm.

Donnie knew where she was. Other than getting wet, there wasn't any real danger if she fell. The trees blocked the moonlight making it difficult to see, but he knew that it was only a five-foot drop. The downside was that she would land in the outlet of a drainage pipe that traveled underneath the road. She would be soaked from the knees down with some very cold water. They would have to abandon the box and abort their mission.

Megan didn't really need his help. If she were alone, she could have propped herself on her elbows and wiggled her way up. There was a chance she would slip and fall backwards, but it was unlikely. Since Donnie was available, she waited for his assistance.

All Megan could see were Donnie's high-top sneakers. Standing between her outstretched arms, he bent at his knees, took hold of Megan by the upper portion of her arms and straightened his legs, thereby hoisting her up and out of her predicament.

She exhaled a big breath like she had done all the work and patted herself off. "Thank you."

"No sweat."

The moonlight came from behind Donnie, casting him in a silhouette and hiding his features from Megan. Megan's face was a little easier to make out, but not much because Donnie's tall body cast a shadow upon her.

Until he met her, the future had been filled with uncertainty. Megan added purpose to his life. He would not have enjoyed going to the mall or purchasing a baseball hat and tambourine before she came to Haviland. It was hard for him to take pleasure in the mundane, knowing that his father couldn't find gratification in anything. But being at the mall, being part of their threesome, he felt involved. For the first time since losing his father, he was part of something.

Seldom did he interact with other people, and they – for the most part – left him alone. He felt unworthy of any affection that Megan showed him, but never for long. She was the only person to make him feel like he deserved it.

To prevent a potentially awkward moment in the middle of their clandestine operation, Megan walked past Donnie and toward the table.

"Let's hurry," she said, "before they realize they forgot something and drive back for it."

Donnie caught up and lifted the front end of the box, while Megan lifted the back. They walked the rest of the way to the storage unit without further incident.

Donnie wanted to open the box and test the table out. Megan wanted to get back.

"My parents are home, you know?" she said. "Sleeping in a bed not far from my own *empty* bed."

"Can we at least stop at Swifts? Grab a couple of hot chocolates for the walk home?"

Swifts was only a block in the wrong direction, but it seemed like a fair compromise. "K," she said. "We stop for one hot cocoa and one decaf coffee. Then straight home."

"Gotcha."

THIRTEEN

It was great to finally have some furniture in Unit #143. The table and two chairs were placed in the center of the unit. Megan put her bookstand on the table, along with some candles. Donnie arranged a few of the larger three-wick candles on the floor at the back of the room. After that, he stepped on one of the chairs and affixed the lampshade upside-down to the bare bulb. The combined effect of the lampshade and candles warmed the mood of the unit. The boom box was placed on a third chair. The streamers from Megan's birthday remained hanging and gave Unit #143 a constant festive atmosphere.

With their backs against the door, they admired their handiwork.

"Look how cozy it looks," Megan said.

"It's definitely an improvement."

Using her right incisor, Megan tugged at her lower lip, "I think we need drapes."

"Don't we need windows to have drapes?"

"Come on, Donnie. Think outside the box."

"Funny."

"What?"

"That's what it is," he said, holding his hands out toward the storage unit. "One big box."

The big box was no longer a barren concrete cell. Not only was it filling up with furniture and effects, it was also accumulating memories. Unit #143 possessed character. It had transformed into a hip hangout.

As their sophomore year waned, Megan became one of Friendly's best servers. She was popular with both families and high school kids. The families liked her because she was fast, efficient, and patient. High school girls liked her because she didn't meddle in their affairs and kept a cool attitude with them. The high school boys liked her because they got to interact with a pretty girl who had no choice but to talk to them.

The weather began to improve and so did business at Dirt's driving range. The air still had a cool, spring crispness to it, but when the sun was out in full, its heat nullified any chill and gave golfers who had been itching to practice their swing a chance to get out.

Donnie enjoyed those sunny days. The mindless monotony of picking up golf balls in an open field was relaxing. It was comforting to know that he was alone, but, at the same time, part of something bigger. He was an important piece of the driving range cycle.

He was also taking more interest in the sport. When things slowed down, Dirt gave him a bucket of balls to hit. Donnie had never seen Dirt swing a golf club, but that didn't keep him from shouting advice from the shack.

"Follow through," he would yell at Donnie, along with, "Keep that left arm straight," and "How many times do I have to tell you to keep your head down? If you look up to see where the ball went, it's still gonna be at your feet."

The biggest difference between practicing his golf swing and practicing for his driver's test was instead of Dirt nagging him, it was his mother: "Slow. Slower. Slow down. Slow down. Slow down!" At least Dirt was more descriptive with his criticism.

Megan's mom offered a minimal amount of driving tips. It was more important to her that she was spending time with her daughter than providing a lesson. Megan had to ask for instruction.

"Mom, it's a one-way street. Can I turn left on red?"

To which Mrs. Priddy would reply, "Do you feel like Thai tonight? Let's stop at the store. Your father won't like it, but he's having dinner at the club."

Despite the inadequacies of their instructors, both of them successfully passed their driver's exams and earned their licenses.

Megan's first trip alone in the car was to the nearest drive-thru for a small fry and diet cola. Her next stop was the discount retailer. She anticipated the summer heat and bought a cooler to keep their beverages cold and snacks from melting in the storage unit.

"Ugh," she said, slouching in her folding chair.

Haviland High released students two hours early on the last day of school. The spring air felt great and it was a beautiful day. At the risk of being seen lounging around their unit, they left the garage door open.

"I can't believe that I agreed to work on the last day of school," she moaned. "The last thing I want to be doing is serving ice cream."

"What would you rather do?"

"Anything!" Megan told him, slouching down even farther. "In my first hours of freedom, I have to work. That sucks."

"It's not that big a deal. Do you work tomorrow?"

"No."

"See. There'll be lots of days this summer that you don't work."

"Still sucks." She thought for a minute. "What the hell are we going to do in here all summer?"

Megan carried her Friendly's uniform in a pale green gym bag as Donnie walked her to work. She would change her clothes in the restroom and put her hair in a ponytail before her shift started.

Donnie always walked her to work if she was leaving from the storage unit. Megan's co-workers began to wonder if they were going together. When the girls asked, Megan never answered with a definitive answer. Her standard reply was a mischievous grin accompanied with a shoulder shrug. She couldn't say because she really didn't know how to describe their relationship and it was none of their business.

Before going home for dinner, Donnie went out of his way to go to the library. He had an idea for how to pass time in the storage unit that summer.

He worked until two o'clock on the first full day of summer vacation. Afterwards, he hooked up with Megan and they walked to Unit #143.

Even though school was out, he had his notebook with him. For years he had carried a notebook from class to class. It was usually a five-subject notebook, but his notes never went deeper than the first three or four pages of each subject. He'd tear a few sheets out here and there to complete homework assignments, but that was about it.

Ten days after his father died, when Donnie returned to school, he had difficulties focusing on the teachers' lessons. Actually, he had difficulties listening to what anyone said. He couldn't go more than a minute without thinking about his father. When he did think of something else, it was always something silly like why is sugar pronounced "shooger" when there's no "h" in it? These thoughts continuously rattled around in his brain and never came to a conclusion. To make matters worse, they continuously spiraled off in new directions. His thoughts and ideas became complicated and intertwined to the extent that it was extremely frustrating.

To appear as though he was taking notes during class, Donnie began writing some of these thoughts in his notebook. Surprisingly, this gave him a sense of relief. He rarely went back to reread what he had written, but by writing it down, it was out of his brain. His mind was clear the next time a random thought about his father or something else attacked him.

His notebook became an ongoing place for him to put whatever came to mind on paper. If it was his dad, he'd write that. If it was the cafeteria menu, he'd add that (the menu was one of the things that he'd refer to later). Sometimes it might be a poem. Sometimes it was an idea such as flavored pen caps. Megan was always chewing her pen cap. What if they came in flavors? He recorded all of these thoughts to keep his mind from exploding.

He was on his fourth notebook since his father's suicide. It was in his backpack when they stopped at Swifts before going to Unit #143.

They purchased a bag of ice and a few bottles of soda. There was a new flavor of Polar Slurp, Orange 'n Cream, which Donnie couldn't pass up trying.

Once in the storage unit, they put their purchases away and Donnie took a plastic case from his backpack.

Megan asked, "What's that?"

Donnie opened the package and inspected the cassettes inside. "It's an audio book."

Donnie had checked it out of the library the day before. He usually read while Megan finished her schoolwork. During the summer, she wouldn't have any.

"We're going to listen to a book?" She was skeptical.

"Uh-huh."

Donnie crouched down in front of the boom box. The only two functions they had ever used were the radio and the CD player and they no longer used the CD player because it burned up batteries too fast.

"What book is it?" Megan asked.

"*Watership Down*."

"Never heard of it."

"It's by Richard Adams."

"Never heard of him."

"Well, I think you're going to like it."

"Why? Have you read it?"

"No." He put tape one into the boom box and closed the cassette door. "I just have a good feeling about it."

"What's it about?"

"Rabbits."

"Rabbits?"

"Well, I know you like rabbits."

"I don't like rabbits."

"You don't?"

She bounced her head back and forth. "I do, but they're not my favorite."

Donnie stood up and tapped the side of his head, trying to jar the right information loose. He snapped his fingers and pointed at Megan, "Pigs!"

"Yes, Donnie. Pigs are my favorite."

"I got confused. Tell me again," he said sitting down with her at the table, "why do you like pigs?"

She answered like he had asked what shape the Earth is, "They're cute!" A true smile of pleasure spread across her face and her eyes glimmered. It was like she was the light bulb above them and someone removed the shade. Megan held her hands apart like she was holding a football by the ends. "Those little ones," she said, "with their little legs and those cute snouts - they're just so a-dor-able." She didn't want Donnie to think that they were just cute animals without substance, so she added, "They're smart, too."

"Really?"

"Uh-huh."

"We'll have to get *Animal Farm* next."

"That's about pigs?"

"Not really. I mean, *Watership Down* isn't really about rabbits either. They're just, um," he took off his baseball cap and scratched his head.

Megan loved when he did this. She got a kick out of how Donnie actually scratched his head when he was thinking. She also liked it anytime his bushy head of black hair was revealed.

"The medium!" he finally said. "The rabbits are the medium through which the story is told."

"You mean like an allegory?"

"Maybe." School was out and he didn't want to think about what allegory meant.

She sipped her diet root beer and said, "Play it."

Donnie went to the boom box and pressed play.

When side one of the first cassette ended, Donnie asked for Megan's opinion by raising his eyebrows.

"That's pretty good," she said.

"So you like the story?"

"I was talking about my root beer."

"Oh." Donnie was disappointed.

"I'm joshin'. I like the story. A lot. What are we going to do? Like a chapter a day or a side a day?"

He was delighted. "As much as we feel like, I guess."

"I like it and it's kind of cool, you know? It's like the old days, before TV. Didn't people sit around and listen to stories on the radio? That's what this is like. Boffo idea, Donnie."

———————————

FOURTEEN

Megan parked her family's blue mini-van and walked around the brown shack with the black saltbox roof. They were going to walk to Unit #143 after dinner, but she felt like seeing Donnie now. She timed it so she would get there when his shift ended at three o'clock. They could load his bike in the van and drive back.

There were two golfers in tee boxes at the far end of the lane. Through her sunglasses, Megan's eyes scanned the open range. She didn't see Donnie out there.

She turned toward the shack to ask his employer where he was, but once she got a look at him, she decided not to. Guys like him didn't live in houses or apartments. They lived in caves or under bridges.

Careful to avoid eye contact with Dirt, she scuttled toward the other end of the small, open-air tee boxes. The golfer nearest Megan picked up his empty basket and passed her on the decaying sidewalk. Without him obstructing her view, she saw that the other golfer was Donnie.

She had no clue that he had taken up golfing. From the way his ball traveled, long and straight, she guessed that he had been practicing all winter. Her father golfed a minimum of twice a week and his favorite thing to discuss with his family when he wasn't on the course was golf. Long and straight was how he desired to strike his ball, but he didn't always succeed at it.

Golf was an individual sport; Donnie liked being alone. Golf involved subtleties that needed to be studied and learned; Donnie was a quiet observer. Golf required patience; Donnie never rushed and only said or did things when he felt ready. It was logical that he would be a natural at golf.

Megan stood partially behind him and partially to his side. She purposely did not make herself more noticeable, but even if she did, Donnie still may not have seen her. He was focused on his activity.

She watched, mesmerized by his actions. Donnie's body was long and tall. His backswing was slow and fluid. Once the club was above his head and perfectly parallel to the ground, he began to pull it back around. This was a fast action. His long arms whipped the club head around, creating a rapid swooshing noise. CLACK! The ball elevated high off the ground and out into the distance. Donnie's head remained down at the tee for nearly a full second before he looked for the flight of the ball.

It landed almost two hundred yards away, bounced a few times, and rolled to a stop. Donnie teed up another ball. His body went through the same progressions and another golf ball was sent flying.

"You're pretty good at that," Megan said as he prepared for another shot.

He neither startled nor turned around. Megan couldn't tell if he had known she was there all along or not. "Thank you. It's all about timing." He sent another ball off before he turned to her and asked, "What are you doing here?"

"I have the van so I thought that I'd give you a ride back."

"Thanks." He turned back around and teed up another golf ball. "Can I finish the bucket? Only a few left."

"Depends. Do I have to help you pick them up?"

He grinned and shook his head. "No. I'll get 'em tomorrow."

There was a precision to Donnie's movements that she had never seen before. His actions usually seemed so awkward and aloof. To watch him, focused on one purpose, was captivating. His aura radiated an energy that tingled her sixth sense and demanded her attention. Megan could have watched Donnie hit golf balls all day. Instead, they went home when his basket was empty.

Later that evening, they walked to the storage unit and listened to *Watership Down*.

When they came to a good stopping point, they put the story on pause and walked to Swifts to replenish their supplies. The cooler was bare.

Along with beverages and snacks, Megan got two packs of playing cards and Donnie bought two boxes of chalk, one white and one colored.

When they got back to Unit #143, Megan turned on the radio and removed the cellophane wrappers from her playing cards.

Donnie asked, "Up or down?"

Megan knew that he was inquiring about the garage door. "Leave it up. It's hot."

He picked the box of white chalk off the table.

"What are you doing with that?"

"Stand over here," he said and pointed to the wall behind his chair.

Megan trusted that it was for a good reason. She got up and walked over.

"Here," he said, gently positioning her body with her back against the concrete block wall. "Sort of...," he began arranging her arms, "with this up maybe, then put this hand out like this..." She stood with her left arm in the air like she was waving to someone far away. Her right hand was a foot away from her waist. "Just stay like that."

"Don't tell me you've taken up knife throwing."

He tossed his Pirates hat on the table. "This will just take a minute. Less than a minute."

Donnie took a piece of white chalk from its box. He bent down and pressed it against the wall on the outside of Megan's right foot. Taking his time and being careful with his line, Donnie began to trace her body.

Megan stood still in her blue denim overall shorts. She stared straight ahead.

Donnie followed the contour of her right leg, past her waistline and up her torso. Tiny bits of chalk dust floated down to the ground.

His right hand held the chalk and the chalk never left the wall. When he reached her right arm, he followed it, traveling back down toward the ground like he was on a switchback.

Through the corner of her right eye, Megan peeked at him. She watched as Donnie rounded her hand, passed the bracelet that he had given her for her birthday, and headed back toward the top of her body.

He slowly drew a line over her bicep and around the curve of her delicate shoulder.

Her shoulder led to her desirable neck. Long and thin and smooth and a perfect cream color. Donnie had never realized how gorgeous a neck could be.

He stopped. The chalk remained against the wall, but his line came to a halt. Her hair, Megan Priddy's trademark red/blonde-blonde/red, delicious orange 'n cream candy-colored hair, tickled the top of Donnie Betts's hand. His lungs froze. He stared at the point where her hair made contact with his hand. So this is what it felt like, he thought. And this is what it looks like when I'm touching it. His head tilted to one side and he regained a slow, methodic breath.

Donnie's eyes never left the piece of chalk. Megan's eyes didn't leave Donnie. His hand slowly resumed moving. More hair fell over his hand. His breath quickened. Involuntarily, he licked his lips as he thought about how her hair would taste. Surely it would melt in his mouth and taste better than cotton candy.

Megan watched him explore every bit of her body. Instead of feeling self-conscious, she felt fabulous. She heard the dull scratch of the chalk scraping the concrete go from one ear to the other as he rounded her head. Her lips fell open and her eyelids grew heavy. The moment was turning into a dream.

The chalk outline traveled down the other side of her neck and across Megan's left shoulder. Donnie silently said goodbye to her gorgeous hair. He wanted to turn back. He wanted to retrace that same line just to experience those marvelous tresses again, but he continued.

Megan's outstretched left arm took Donnie away from the trunk of her body. With his generous height, he had no difficulties following her arm to her hand, where he lingered to inspect the rings on her thumb and middle finger before heading back toward her body.

Since he was using his right hand and tracing the left side of her body, Donnie was very close to Megan. He couldn't keep himself from staring at her breasts since they were directly in front of him. That made him think of the mannequins dressed in nothing but bras and panties at the mall.

And down he went. Down past her groovalicious belly and alluring hips. Down her left leg. Down, down, down as a Ramones tune beat from the boom box's speakers.

When he reached her foot, he uttered, "Almost there."

Donnie briefly pulled the piece of chalk off the wall and placed it on the inside of her foot. He traveled back up toward the center of her body.

Megan's relaxed breath journeyed deeper inside of her. Her chest expanded with large gulps of air as she anticipated the path his hand would follow.

Past her knee. Past her smooth thighs.

Delicately, oh so delicately, Donnie traced the curve of her most private area. He was careful not to come in contact with denim, but he didn't shy away from making an accurate outline.

Back down he went, one final time.

A thin layer of powdery white dust covered the floor beneath Megan. They would need to buy a broom.

Donnie stood straight up. Megan took hold of his T-shirt with her right hand and held him there so he could not get away. She held him until he looked down into her pineapple-leaf green eyes and when he did, she kissed him.

At age sixteen, Donnie Betts helped Megan Priddy discover lust. She placed her left hand on the back of his neck and kissed him again. Longer this time.

When they stopped to catch their breath, Megan looked from one side of the unit to the other. Her eyes settled on the radio.

She hypothesized, "I think the Ramones turn me on."

FIFTEEN

The next day, Donnie's shift at work ended before Megan's, but Megan was the first to arrive at Unit #143. She used the privacy to change out of her Friendly's uniform and into a yellow and blue pastel flowered summer dress.

Donnie rode up on his mountain bike nearly half an hour after Megan finished changing her clothes. Beads of perspiration rolled down his forehead and dripped from his face.

"Hey," he said, dumping his backpack on a chair and moving straight to the cooler for a refreshment. His T-shirt was a deeper shade of green from the sweat where his backpack had been pressing against him. It clung uncomfortably to his back. He yanked a towel from his backpack and wiped his face off.

"Hi," Megan replied as casually as she could.

Neither spoke after that, but it wasn't for a lack of having anything to say.

Megan enjoyed being open with Donnie. She could explore her thoughts out loud or just say silly stuff that made little sense without being judged by him. This was the first time that Megan had difficulties speaking what was on her mind. Part of the problem of telling Donnie what she was thinking was that she wasn't entirely clear about what it was.

For the past half hour, she had been sitting and looking at the chalk outline of herself on the wall. After the kiss ended and before they left, Donnie had added a mixture of red, pink, and yellow to the outline for a very rough approximation of her hair. She insisted that he draw the bracelet around her wrist as well. It was strange looking at a life-size tracing of her body.

Starting where Donnie first pressed the chalk against the wall, Megan followed the contour of the line. Silently and alone, she relived each exhilarating moment. She imagined Donnie in front of her, carefully moving along the curves of her body with the chalk.

Then she closed her eyes and thought about the kiss. Her impression at the time was that Donnie enjoyed it as much as she did. He tasted better than a Rice Krispie treat, but it wasn't just his lips that gave her bliss. They physically shared something emotional. It was a new sensation that she had thought about all night, until she fell asleep with a smile of contentment smeared across her face.

The next morning she awoke with the same tingling sensation, but an unease now accompanied it. The excitement of the kiss lingered on her lips for her entire shift at Friendly's that day. The question of whether it was the right thing to do haunted her during that same period. She was torn. She didn't want to encourage anything that might cause a strain on their relationship.

She valued Donnie's friendship more than any possession. He was dependable. He was caring, fun, and understanding. He listened to her and took a sincere interest in everything that she did. His dry wit made her laugh. He gave her space when she needed it but still managed to always be there for her at the right time. Donnie Betts was everything that her father wasn't.

He even let her read some of the beautiful thoughts that he recorded in his notebook. He only let her look at a few pages and not for very long, but it was like watching the favorite part of her favorite movie.

When he pulled the cover to one side and exposed the pages inside, he was opening up more than just the notebook.

It was a random blend of scribbles that only made sense in its entirety to him. Some of it was like poetry where the lines ran together and some of it was like dialogue from a play. All of it tugged at her heart or made her laugh. One page was filled with the word "away" written over and over again. Saying it or thinking it seemed meaningless, but when that one word was repeated on a piece of paper from top to bottom, it was spellbinding.

She watched as Donnie rehydrated and caught his breath. He ran a hand through his hair and trapped the sweaty mop underneath his baseball cap. He sniffed once and scratched his arm. At that moment, he became irresistibly attractive. She wanted to kiss him right then. She wanted nothing more than to hold and kiss a very sweaty and dirty boy. Had she lost her mind?

She wondered if Donnie desired the same thing. Maybe he viewed their kiss as a mistake. Possibly, he regretted it. It could be that he wanted to pretend that it never happened. It could be that he wanted everything to return to the way it was.

Megan studied his face. No one could read Donnie's countenance better than she. Actually, the only other person who could read it at all was his mother. Megan looked at it for signs of what he wanted, but beyond quenching his thirst, she saw nothing. She knew Donnie though. He was an expert at hiding his emotions. She could tell from the crinkle in the corner of his eyes and the way he kept his lips pushed together that something was going on inside him. She just couldn't decipher what it was.

He'd eventually tell her what was on his mind. He always did. He just never did it before he was ready. This time she couldn't wait. There was too much going on inside of her. Honesty was the cornerstone of their friendship, but this was a situation they had never encountered.

So just tell him, she thought. Or better yet, just kiss him again!

She held back. She restrained herself. Why? She didn't know. Then she figured it out. Donnie's heart was fragile. After losing someone whom he loved so very much to suicide, did Donnie still have any love of his own to give away?

It scared her. She was afraid of hurting Donnie, unintentionally, of course. What if a romantic relationship wasn't right for them? She couldn't take the chance. Megan didn't want to force Donnie into something that he wasn't ready for. She did love him. What else could that feeling be? Megan had fallen in love with adorable Donnie.

More and more questions kept popping up. STOP! she silently yelled at herself. Megan refused to take the chance of hurting Donnie. If their relationship was to go forward romantically, he would have to be the one to make the next move. Even if that's what he wanted, it could take an eternity. He always made certain that he wanted something before acting upon it. Megan would keep her feelings to herself. It went against everything they based their friendship on, but there was no other way. She could never forgive herself if she caused Donnie pain.

"I bought a poster," he said, setting his drink down on the table. He pulled a tube of paper wrapped in plastic from his backpack.

"What is it?" Megan asked.

Keeping his head down, Donnie smiled. He quickly pulled it back to a grin and then, before he looked up, the elation was gone from his face.

He was up to something, she thought. That's good. He smiled. He's over yesterday. She wouldn't have to dwell on it anymore. He's moving on and I should, too.

He poked a hole through the plastic at the hollow end of the tube and slid the poster out. In a couple of quick, long strides, he was at the wall opposite Megan's chalk outline.

"Look away," he said.

"What?"

"C'mon. Just do it."

She obliged.

Megan could hear the poster being unraveled, followed by the sound of packing tape, presumably clear, ripping from its roll.

A minute later, Donnie said, "OK."

She turned and looked. Before her was a black and white poster of four guys hanging out at the corner of Bowery and Leeker Street. Red capital letters in the upper left-hand corner of the poster read: RAMONES.

Megan blushed and her freckles darkened. Donnie stood next to the poster, beaming at her. There was no question about how he felt now.

Kissing in Unit #143 became a regular activity for Donnie and Megan that summer. Positioning themselves for it was difficult. They either had to stand or push two chairs together. Neither was a comfortable necking position for very long.

They listened to *Watership Down* on cassette regularly and it did not take them long to finish.

"That was a good ending," she said on the day the last bit of the final chapter played. "Those rabbits really had to stick together."

"Yeah, it was a good book," Donnie agreed. He fast-forwarded the cassette to the end, removed it, and turned on the radio.

"At first I wasn't sure if I'd like how they had those stories, you know those folk tales they were telling all the time, inside the real story. But they were just as cool." She took out the two decks of cards. "Who was your favorite character? I liked the bird."

"Yeah, he was a big help." Donnie tapped the skin of his tambourine. The little cymbals jingled. "I liked Fiver."

"Really?"

"Yeah. Fiver was the one who had the vision. He was the reluctant hero. He kept them going. How could you not dig Fiver?"

"I didn't say I didn't," Megan was slightly defensive.

Donnie put the pack of tapes in his backpack. "When I take this back, I'll pick up another one."

"Can you wait a week on that?"

"Sure. Why?"

"I'd like to read *Charlie and the Chocolate Factory*. Can I borrow your copy?" She thought that he might say "no" since his copy held strong sentimental value. If that were the case, she could buy her own on the Internet.

"I'd love for you to borrow it."

"Thanks." She smiled. Donnie kissed her. He couldn't resist. "All right, c'mon lover boy," she said, playfully admonishing him. "Let's play double solitaire."

"Play what?"

"Double solitaire."

"What is that? Can't we play blackjack or, better yet, chess?" This was an inside joke. During the school year, they sometimes told their parents that they were staying after school because they were in the chess club. No such club existed and, if it did, it certainly wouldn't meet as often as they said it did.

"Sit down," she told him. "I'll teach you. It's not hard. You know how to play solitaire, right?"

"Not without a computer."

"You're kidding?"

He shook his head.

Megan rolled her eyes and exhaled loudly, purposely making a big show of it. She shuffled and dealt the cards so she could go over the rules that Donnie needed clarification on. Once it was clear that he understood the basic rules of regular solitaire, she picked the cards up and tossed him the second deck.

"K," she said, "it's just like regular solitaire. You deal your game and I deal mine. The only difference is that we share aces."

"What do you mean?"

"Like if I put the ace of hearts up, you can put your two of hearts on top of it."

"Oh, all right."

"We only win if we both get all of our cards up."

They played for over an hour. When they finished it was dark outside. Donnie pulled his chair to the edge of the unit and Megan joined him.

"I wish we could see more stars," he said.

Megan observed the sky. She counted about ten. "I never really thought about it," she said. "There's usually more than that. Aren't there?"

"Way more. They're there. We just can't see them from all the light pollution."

"We should plan a field trip, you know? Drive way out into some real rural area so we can see all the stars. Let's do it."

"Right now?"

"No, but soon."

"All right."

They held hands and searched the sky for anything unusual.

"That star is real bright," Megan literally pointed it out.

"It's probably a planet."

"Don't we need a telescope for that?"

"Uh-uh."

"Crazy. I didn't know that. Which one is it?"

"I don't know. Venus, maybe?"

"We'll need like an astronomy book or something for our field trip so we know what's what."

Donnie shrugged. "I suppose."

"Yeah, that'll be cool."

The Ramones came on. Megan gave Donnie a sidelong glance. Any Ramones song always provoked the same response – a French kiss.

They didn't have to wait a week to go to the library. Megan finished *Charlie and the Chocolate Factory* in only three days.

They met in the street between their houses to go to the library. Donnie had his bike. Megan did not.

"Let's take our bikes," Donnie urged. "It's not far."

"Nah. I've got the van. My mom's not going anywhere all day. C'mon, I'll drive." She moved closer to him. "We don't have to come straight home after the library, you know? The van has a comfortable back seat."

"Comfortable?"

It wasn't really that comfortable. "More so than the chairs that came with the card table."

Donnie turned and walked his bike to the garage. Megan waited for him. They walked across the street together and got in the Priddys' blue mini-van. Before they pulled out of Megan's driveway, her mother rushed to the passenger side door.

Megan said, "Oh boy," as Donnie powered down the window.

"Hi, Donnie. How are you?" Megan's mom cheerily inquired.

"Good, Mrs. Priddy."

"Good! How are things at the driving range?"

"It's all good."

"Megan tells me that you have a good swing."

"I guess."

"You may need to give Mr. Priddy some lessons!"

"I doubt that."

Megan flipped through a book of CDs that she had taken from her bedroom.

Donnie fiddled with the ends of his shorts and then adjusted his baseball cap.

Megan's mom stood silently outside the car. Her smile was constant, like a five-year-old home from her trip to the dentist and proud of her no-cavities report.

Megan found the CD she wanted to listen to and was ready to go. "Mom?" she said impatiently.

"Yes, honey?"

"What do you want?"

"Donnie looks good in that hat. Don't you think?"

Megan always played off how good she thought Donnie looked in his Pirates hat. This time, she replied, "I think he looks hot in it."

Donnie's head whipped to his left to see if Megan was serious or being sarcastic. Her impish grin achieved what she wanted. Donnie was unable to decipher the true intention of her statement.

Mrs. Priddy set her hands on the door and said to Donnie, "We'd like to have you and your mother over for dinner on Saturday. Do you guys already have plans?"

Donnie and his mother never had plans. They never did anything together. She worked every other Saturday night at 10:00. The upcoming Saturday was a night off.

"Um, no... We don't have plans. Ah, I'll... I'll ask her when we get back."

"Super-fantastic. I can't believe that I haven't met her yet. I bet that she's a great mother! She raised such a wonderful son."

Megan yelled, "Mom!" and turned the music on full blast. "Gotta go!" Donnie, who was sitting right next to her, could barely hear her voice over the wailing guitars.

After they pulled into the street, Donnie turned the music down and said, "You could have warned me that was coming."

"I had no idea," she pleaded. "In fact, it's really strange. Saturday nights are my mom's only night out alone with my dad."

"Never mind that," Donnie said. "How's her cooking?"

SIXTEEN

"The Priddys invited us to dinner Saturday night," Donnie informed his mother later that evening.

She answered, "I have to work Saturday."

Donnie sat at the small table in the long but narrow kitchen of their home. His mother prepared their dinner on the counter next to the stove. It was nearly 9:00 at night.

"Close the book, Donnie, and get us a couple sodas."

Donnie shut his book, placed it on top of his notebook, and shoved them against the wall to make room for his plate.

"You don't work this Saturday," he said, pulling a two-liter from the refrigerator. "You just worked this past Saturday."

"Oh, I meant that I'm busy this Saturday."

"OK," Donnie was skeptical. "What are you doing?"

"I'm going bowling."

She put their plates of tacos on the table and he set the drinks down. They both sat. Neither spoke as they wolfed down their first two tacos. Without saying anything, his mother placed a third taco on each of their plates.

When she sat back down, Donnie said, "It's just that Megan is my best friend and I thought that it would be kind of cool to, um… They're new here, so they don't know… They never knew him so they probably… It won't feel like they're judging us."

Mrs. Betts's chewing slowed to a near stop.

Donnie continued, "I'd like to go. I like her. It's nice to have friends and do stuff. I think that it might be fun. I'm going. I'd like it if you came too. Do you understand?"

She wasn't going bowling on Saturday. She rarely left the house for anything but work or groceries. Now that Donnie had his driver's license, she seldom even made the trip to the store. Bowling was a poor, phony excuse that she blurted to get out of going.

"It's only across the street," Donnie said.

The throbbing pain left by her husband's suicide interfered with her ability to properly parent her only child. The best way to dull the pain was to ignore it. The only way to do that was to stop caring. She couldn't isolate her husband's death from everything else so she would stop caring about everything. This would last anywhere from a day to a week. Laundry would pile up and she would oversleep. When she snapped out of it, she became overprotective of Donnie. She worried about her son's happiness and losing him. Then the day would come again when it hurt too much and she'd revert to not caring.

She was currently suffering through a careless phase, but Donnie's polite encouragement pulled her from the fog and helped her remember the importance of her son.

Donnie walked to the refrigerator to get more soda for them. With his back turned to her, she sighed. "Ask Mrs. Priddy what time she would like us and tell her that we'll bring dessert."

He closed the refrigerator. "Thanks, mom."

On Saturday, their roles were reversed. Since their shifts did not coincide, Donnie hadn't seen Megan all day. She let him know on Friday that they would be grilling out, something her father claimed he loved to do but never did. Not seeing Megan before going over that evening made Donnie nervous. With each passing minute, the Priddy house across the street appeared more ominous. He never felt awkward around Megan, but around strangers, he usually did.

Donnie's mother noticed his anxiety and asked, "What's the matter?"

"What if something goes wrong?"

"Like what?"

"I don't know. If I knew, I could prepare for it and nothing would be the matter."

"It will be fine, Donnie. I'm sure they'll make us feel at home."

This thought was only somewhat comforting. He didn't necessarily like how he felt at home. Depending on his mother's mood, he either felt ignored or like revered royalty. He desired consistency.

When it was time, they walked across the street with their dessert.

The inside of the Priddy home was like a museum, not because it housed rare artifacts or extravagant artwork (although they did have a few nice pieces) but because of the meticulous arrangement of everything. Donnie didn't know how they lived there. He was afraid to walk on the carpet or upset the neatness of the room. He didn't feel comfortable until he was ushered to the only spot that he was familiar with, the deck in the backyard.

He didn't feel comfortable there for long, either. Megan's father was preparing the grill. He definitely did his shopping in the big and tall man's section of the store because he was both.

When he saw Donnie, he set down the grill brush. Mr. Priddy wiped his hands off with a towel and rested them on his hips before saying, "So here's the Donnie Betts that's been running around with my daughter all summer."

"No, sir," Donnie replied. "I'm the Donnie Betts that lives across the street. I've heard about that other one, though. Real unsavory character." Nothing like breaking the ice with a joke, right?

Mr. Priddy's response was a brief laugh that sounded like a gun shot through a silencer, "Heh." He looked Donnie over for a few seconds before shaking his hand. "Nice to meet you, Donnie." Donnie's weak grip left an unfavorable first impression on him.

When Donnie's mother commented on how nice their house was, Mrs. Priddy insisted on giving her a tour.

"Would you like to come along, Donnie?" Mrs. Priddy asked.

He didn't see the point in looking at other people's homes, but recognized it as an opportunity to get away from Mr. Priddy and regroup. Before he got the chance to reply, Megan answered for him.

"Maybe later," she said and discreetly winked in his direction.

Mrs. Priddy and Mrs. Betts went inside.

"Want something to drink?" Megan asked him.

"Sure."

"Are you twenty-one?" her father asked.

"No."

Mr. Priddy pointed with his spatula to a red cooler with a white top. "Help yourself to anything but the beer."

Until that evening, Megan had forgotten how shy Donnie could be. When alone with him in Unit #143, Donnie told stories and joked around. He spoke his mind more freely. At dinner, he didn't offer any more than he had to. That's not to say that he still wasn't charming.

Megan could tell that her mother was enamored by him; however, it was also obvious to her that her father was skeptical of him, but she didn't know why. That didn't bother her, though. She didn't need her father's approval to date Donnie. The guy was hardly around.

Donnie was the model of politeness. When asked questions, he didn't just shake his head no or nod his head yes. He answered with complete sentences and full thoughts. Occasionally, he would make a few subtle jokes, but Megan seemed to be the only one there who understood his humor. Maybe Mrs. Betts did, but she never showed an appreciation for it.

Donnie was surprised by how much his mother interacted with the Priddys. He wished that she would stay that way forever. He considered that for a moment and changed his mind. He preferred that she act at the Priddys' the way she acted at home. That was his true mother these days.

When dinner was over, Megan said, "I'm going to give Donnie that tour now."

"That's nice, honey," her mother replied.

As they traversed the hallways, Donnie asked, "How do you get around in here?"

"What do you mean?"

"Everything is so…," he searched for the right word, "perfect."

"Perfect?"

"Yeah, like everything is right where it should be. Aren't you scared of messing stuff up?"

She laughed at him, "No."

The last stop on the tour was Megan's bedroom. She walked inside. Donnie stayed in the doorway.

"What's up?" she said. "I thought you'd be excited to see my room."

"I am, but," his long arm reached behind his ear where he scratched a non-existent itch, "I sort of have this vision of it.

I kind of have a picture in my mind of how it should look and, um… I don't… I like my interpretation."

"Screw your interpretation," she said taking his hand. "This is the real thing!" She walked him inside.

The room was two things: purple and white.

The walls were a soft yet vibrant shade of purple. The carpet and the ceiling were white. All the trim, doors, and closets were white. The bookcase with hinged doors and the nightstand were white. Her desk was white. The bed was white, but the comforter was purple. There were two lamps. They were white with purple shades. Even the clock/radio's numbers were purple.

What was even more amazing was that those two colors were almost all that he saw. He knew that she had CDs and schoolbooks in the room, but they weren't anywhere to be seen. Everything that wasn't purple or white was neatly hidden away.

"You like it?" she said.

Donnie realized that he had been standing in the middle of her room with his mouth gaping open.

He replied slowly, "Yeah."

"What comes to mind when you see it?"

Donnie went for the obvious, "Purple and white?"

"Yeah! Isn't it great?"

He nodded. Donnie expected some posters on the walls and a few CDs lying around. He thought that he'd see magazine clipping of guys here and some clothes spread out over there. It would be evident to anyone that the room belonged to a teenager, but somehow, it was a very mature room.

"I sleep with pigs every night," she informed him with a smile.

"Really?"

"Yup, look!" She pulled back the comforter to reveal bed sheets covered in pigs. "How cute are they?"

He didn't bother hiding his indifference, "Adorable."

She threw the comforter back down and pulled a picture off of the dresser. The frame was white, but the actual picture was one of the few things in the room that wasn't either purple or white.

She hugged the frame to her chest. The photo inside it was hidden from Donnie's view.

"K, Donnie," she said. "I'm going to show you something now. It's not to be talked about after today."

"I'm ready."

Staring at his face to see his reaction, she flipped the picture around and held it at arm's length. It was of Megan Priddy and two other girls. Megan's hair, straight and without style, was the color of brown smog.

"*That*," she said, "is my natural hair color. What do you think?"

"You're cute."

"Bullshit!" She said it too loud. She covered her mouth and poked her head out the door to make sure no one was around to hear. They were still on the deck. "I'm chunky and my hair is blah."

"Let me see," Donnie said, taking the picture from her. "Well, you're cuter now."

"Yeah?"

"You're older and… well…" He confessed, "Your hair is awesome. I love your hair. The color, the texture, the subtle detail… I mean, when I see you, I want to put my head against yours so I can be closer to it."

"Why don't you?"

"Now?"

Megan's eyebrows crinkled in a "what do you think?" kind of way just before she sung, "Noooo." She wrapped a lock of hair behind her ear. "But if you wanted to nibble on this sometime, I wouldn't stop you."

"Hmm." Donnie's eyes returned to the photo. "Who are the other girls?"

"Friends from my old school. I never talk to them anymore."

"Why are you wearing a jean jacket?"

"Alllll right," she said, grabbing for the picture, "that's enough."

Donnie pulled back so she couldn't take it. "Wait." He inspected the photo again. Something else was different. He looked at the picture, then to Megan, then back at the picture, and then back to Megan again.

She noticed his comparative glances and asked, "What?"

Megan had matured. More specifically, Megan's breasts had matured. They were considerably larger now than when they met. How could he have missed them all this time?

"Nothing," he answered.

SEVENTEEN

Megan's mother called up from the bottom of the staircase, "Kids, finish up and come on down for dessert."

Megan gave Donnie a peck on the cheek and scooted off down the hall. Donnie set the picture down on her desk. From the top of the stairs, Megan called back to him, "C'mon."

He followed her down the steps and out the back door.

The three adults were sitting around the table. The grill was turned off and the plates had been cleared. Donnie was surprised to see a beer in front of his mom. She typically didn't drink, but must have felt obligated to join the Priddys in their consumption of alcohol. Seeing her with a beer brought back memories of his father's heavy drinking. He shoved these thoughts into shadows of his head.

Megan lifted the lid of the cooler and pulled out two root beers.

"What were you kids doing?" Mr. Priddy wanted to know.

"I was just showing him around," Megan said.

"Did you show him your room?" he asked.

"Yup."

Mrs. Priddy asked Donnie, "What did you think?"

"Nice." All of them continued looking at him, expecting more. What could he say? It was solid purple and white. He didn't want to state the evident so he reached for what was out of the ordinary. "The pig bed sheets were cool."

Mr. Priddy's eyes narrowed. "What were you doing looking at the bed sheets?"

"I was showing him the pigs, daddy," Megan explained.

"Hmm," he replied with disapproval.

Donnie's mother began slicing the pie they had brought.

"What flavor is it, Mrs. Betts?" Megan asked, taking her seat at the table.

"Why don't you ask Donnie?"

Three pairs of Priddy eyes fell on Donnie.

Megan officially asked him, "What flavor of pie is it, Donnie?"

His throat dried up like a hamburger under a heat lamp. "Blackberry," he croaked and raised his root beer to his lips.

The Priddy women "ooohh"ed and Mr. Priddy repeated what he heard, "Blackberry."

"Go on, Donnie," his mother prodded. "Where did the berries come from?"

His sip of soda didn't help the dryness. "I picked them."

"Oh really!" Mrs. Priddy said. "Fresh blackberries! How nice is that?"

Megan smiled proudly. It was just like Donnie to do something like pick fresh berries for dessert.

"I just did the picking," Donnie said. "My mother did the rest."

When Donnie's mother began handing out the slices, Megan prompted her, "Just a sliver for me, please."

Mr. Priddy centered his slice of pie in front of him and asked Donnie, "Where did you find them?"

"What?"

"The blackberries."

"Oh, they grow in the woods across the street from my job."

"And where's that?"

"It's a driving range."

Mr. Priddy became more interested in what Donnie had

to say. He set his fork down and asked, "What do you do there?"

"I retrieve golf balls."

Mrs. Betts said, "Honey, I told you this…"

"It's not like the driving range at the country club, dad," Megan said. "He doesn't go around in a cart that automatically picks up the balls when he drives over them. Donnie manually picks each one up."

"Does that get exhausting?" Mrs. Priddy asked.

"I don't mind it," Donnie said.

"He's a good golfer, too," Megan added. "How far can you drive the ball, Donnie?"

"Oh, um…" Donnie was reluctant to speak about his golfing skills. "I'm not really a good golfer. I've never been off the range. I wouldn't know what to do on a real course…"

"Don't be modest," Mr. Priddy dared him. "How far can you drive the ball?"

Donnie shrugged as if he wasn't sure, "Two-hundred yards?"

"At least!" Megan said.

"Is that good?" Donnie's mom asked. She didn't know that Donnie used the driving range to practice. She just thought of it as his job.

"Sure, it's good," Megan's dad said. He picked up his fork and went to work on his pie. He spoke in between bites. "Donnie, as you may know, I have two daughters. I love them dearly, but they're not going to do me any good in the upcoming father/son tournament at the club. If I can finagle it so you could play with me…"

Megan and her mother's eyes went wide. It figured that the aloof man in their house wasn't paying attention when they went over the ground rules before the Betts arrived. Megan had explained that they didn't need to tiptoe around the delicate issue surrounding the Betts. Donnie consciously took strides to move forward from the tragedy, but they still needed to be sensitive of his circumstances. How could he have been so careless as to mention something like a father/son tournament to Donnie – the boy whose father killed himself?

Megan's mom tried to cover for her husband's error, "Now honey, Megan's boyfriend just said that he never actually does any real golfing…"

Megan's eyes stretched so wide that they resembled ping pong balls. Boyfriend?!?! She turned to Donnie to see his reaction to her mom's arbitrary label.

He didn't see her because he looked at his mother when she said, "Megan's your girlfriend? I didn't know that."

"Kent Selleck already thinks he's got the tournament wrapped up," Mr. Priddy said, ignoring them. "What he doesn't know is that I have an ace-in-the-hole with you, Donnie-boy."

"They spend all their time together," Mrs. Priddy said to Donnie's mother.

Mrs. Betts then asked Donnie the outrageous, "Have you kissed?"

The flurry of conversation came to an abrupt stop like the silent pause that occurs when a car passes underneath a bridge in a rainstorm.

The rain resumed its onslaught when Mr. Priddy, who apparently was in his own world, opened another beer. He wasn't sure how good Donnie was, but he was the best prospect that he had. He said, "We have time to get in a practice round or two in before the tournament. What do you say, Donnie? Are you free on Wednesday?"

Donnie was on the spot and panicked. "I'd rather not" was the signal his brain sent to his mouth, but somewhere between the two, wires got crossed and he said, "Wednesday's good."

Mr. Priddy held his bottle up in a toast.

Megan buried her face in her hands.

Mrs. Priddy stared at her husband.

And Mrs. Betts said to Donnie, "Why didn't you tell me that Megan is your girlfriend?"

EIGHTEEN

The following day, Donnie and Megan hung out at their storage unit. Megan had a scheduled day off from Friendly's. Donnie was supposed to work, but it had been raining all day. Golfers didn't like the rain.

They played a few hands of double solitaire before putting the cards away. The door was left open so they could watch the storm clouds. Not many people used Parkside Storage on rainy days so they didn't have to worry about their privacy.

"Look at all that rain," Megan said. "I can't believe how much there is."

"And it just keeps coming," Donnie replied. "Kind of like snot."

"Ewwwww. What?"

"Like, you know," he explained, slightly embarrassed and partly proud of his analogy, "when you have a runny nose from a cold. You keep blowing it and blowing it, but there always seems to be more snot. Where does it all come from?"

Megan rolled her eyes and shook her head.

"You get what I'm saying," Donnie said.

Reluctantly, she agreed.

They moved their chairs to the edge of Unit #143. Together, they watched the rain blanket their town. When the frequency of the heavy drops increased, the noise of them smacking down on the roofs and pavement was louder than a fat man wearing neon pink. They kept the radio off and listened to the precipitation.

"Would it be weird for me to say that the rain is beautiful?" Megan asked.

"Nah."

"We always think of warm sunny days with low humidity as beautiful, but look at this." They admired the torrent of rain washing over Haviland. "This is nature being gorgeous in a whole different way."

"Yeah."

They watched the tiny bits of cloud fall to the ground until the worst of the storm moved on, leaving an eerie, unusual light in its wake. It wasn't late enough to be dark out, but it was and everything had a bland tinge of orange surrounding it.

"I'm sorry about all that crap yesterday," Megan told him.

"It's all right."

"You don't have to play golf with my dad. That's crazy."

"We'll see. Actually, I don't have any clubs."

"Why didn't you tell him that?"

"Yeah, I wasn't thinking."

"What do you use at the driving range?"

"Dirt has an extra driver, four iron, and pitching wedge that he lets me use."

She didn't know exactly what that meant but nodded her head anyway.

In the distance, there was a flash of lightning followed by a loud crack and a low boom. Megan jumped at the sound.

"Scare you?" Donnie asked.

"No," she rubbed her arms. "Just gave me goose bumps."

Since they were discussing the previous evening, she thought it was a good time to bring up the other embarrassing topic. "I never told them anything about you being my boyfriend."

Donnie was quiet.

Megan was uncomfortable with his silence and rushed to say more. "It's just something my mom assumed and she must have said something to my dad about it..."

Donnie continued to watch the final drops of rain descend from the sky.

Megan rambled on, "I should have known it was coming. The girls at Friendly's are always asking about you. You know, like they think we're going together or whatever. For the longest time I just shrugged them off, but anymore, I...," she cut herself off. "Donnie?"

He looked at her.

"I wanna be your girlfriend."

Donnie nodded along and said, "I wanna be your boyfriend."

Megan smiled. "That's boffo."

"No. You didn't let me finish," Donnie said. "I was saying: 'I Wanna Be Your Boyfriend' is my favorite Ramones song."

"Oh."

Megan was embarrassed, but Donnie rescued her before long. "I'm kidding."

"Oh." Her smile returned.

"Actually, 'I Believe in Miracles' is my favorite Ramones song, not 'I Wanna Be Your Boyfriend'."

"Oh." Megan's disappointment returned.

Donnie laughed. "I'm just messing with you. Yeah, sure. I don't care what you call us. If you want to label us as boyfriend and girlfriend, that's fine. I'll go along with that. I don't know what it is that I like about you, but I sure like it a lot and giving it a name isn't going to change a thing."

She wrapped her arms around him and kissed him before he could say anything else.

Later in the evening, Megan closely studied the details of her boyfriend's face. He wore his Pirates hat backwards and shaggy black hair escaped through the hole where the adjustable strap was located. His cute chubby cheeks didn't coincide with the rest of his slender body. The afterglow of the storm reflected brilliantly off his eyes. He was more attractive to her now than ever.

Donnie noticed her staring. "What?"

"Can I ask you something?" she asked.

"Anything."

"Does stuff like my dad inviting you to a father/son tournament upset you?"

The rain had stopped, but the runoff continued. Donnie watched the water rush down the alley and into the drain, where its trickle echoed.

"I suppose," he eventually said, "that the word 'father' has negative connotation for me, but it's not something I'd hold against your dad."

"Do you think that will ever go away?"

"What?"

"The pain associated with 'father'."

"I don't know, Megan," his voice was distant. "I don't even know if I want it to."

"What do you mean?"

"Like, I don't want to forget him. I don't want to forget what he did."

"But you shouldn't have to suffer with it forever."

"You think I'm suffering?"

"You did say 'negative connotation'."

"I did," he conceded. "You don't know what it's like. No one possibly can. Even if I tell you about it. Even if I tell you everything, there'll be this intangible stuff left out that you just won't get." Donnie seldom got worked up about anything, but he couldn't keep the tremble from entering his voice. "You know, like you can imagine your dad doing the same thing to put yourself in my shoes. You can pretend just to try to feel what it must be like for me, but in the back of your head, you'll know that you're pretending. That it's not real. That he's really not gone. That he didn't deliberately kill himself. I know. I know because I try to pretend the opposite - that my father is still alive. That doesn't work. It doesn't." He rubbed the top of his head with both hands. His hat fell to the floor and made a gentle clap when it hit the concrete. "There's stuff that no one ever gets. Stuff that I don't want to explain 'cause it'll do no good. Stuff that I can't even explain to myself. The only person who has any answers is me and half the time I can't figure out what the freakin' questions are." He was sobbing but not quite crying.

Megan turned her chair toward his. "What about me, Donnie?"

"What?"

"Do I get you?"

He looked her in the eyes.

Megan took his hands. He thought of the first time that she had grabbed hold of his hand and the warm chill that it sent through his body. Her touch was still magical.

"I think you might," he told her and then shook his head. "I don't know how, but… you got through the wall. I don't know how…"

"Most people probably try climbing it. I just kept looking for the door."

He smiled briefly. "Now that you're in, what're you going to do?"

"Nothing. Just tell me whatever you want to tell me and know that…" She paused. She had to choose the right words. Megan wanted Donnie to know how much he meant to her, but she didn't want to freak him out. "I puppy love you."

"Puppy love." He chuckled after repeating her choice of words. "Yeah."

Donnie took a deep breath and exhaled. "So you want me to tell you stuff about my dad's suicide?"

"Only if you want to."

"I want to. I do. But, I can't. I can't because I don't know how. I mean, I don't know how I feel about it or the right words for how I feel and then it changes every day. I couldn't just say to you what's on my mind because they're just these thoughts that…"

"Shh, shh, shh," Megan cut him off. He was getting worked up again. She pointed toward his backpack. "Is it all in there?"

He knew what she meant. His notebook went everywhere with him. He nodded.

"Can I read it?"

"It's not the only one. I have several of them."

"I'd like to read them all. May I?"

What could he say? She was already on the other side of the wall. He nodded again.

NINETEEN

The driving range was nearly golf ball free when Donnie finally sat down on the bench that leaned against the shack.

Dirt stuck his head out the window and asked in his crackling voice, "Where's your bike, kid?"

"Got a ride today," Donnie said without turning to look at him.

"All summer long you've been riding that freakin' bike."

"Well, not today."

Donnie was waiting for Megan to pick him up. It was the last Saturday before their junior year started and they were taking their planned field trip to get a better view of the stars. Megan had even bought an astronomy book and one of those little lights to clip on it. She gave him a lift to work so they wouldn't have to worry about his bike later on when it was time to drive to the countryside far north of Atlanta.

Donnie heard the side door of the shack close and the scruffy, round man turned the corner with a bag of golf clubs.

"You going golfing, Dirt?" Donnie said. Although he owned a driving range and knew what a good swing looked like, Donnie never knew Dirt to be a golfer.

"No! I hate golf. Damn sport will make a grown man cry. I seen it." He set the tan bag filled with clubs down next to Donnie. "You're still a kid though, so you're in the clear."

"What are you talking about?"

Dirt handed him some cash. "Here's your pay for the day."

"Thanks."

"I noticed you've been gettin' pretty good at swinging the club."

"Despite your coaching."

"Don't be a wiseguy… I thought that you might like taking your game to a real golf course sometime, so I got these for ya." He nodded to the bag of clubs.

"Those are for me?"

"Yeah," Dirt drew the word out. "I would have given them to you a while ago, but you've been on that bike all summer. Can't carry clubs and ride a bike at the same time, can you?"

Donnie answered absentmindedly, "No." He began inspecting the clubs and the bag. "This is awesome, Dirt. Thanks so much."

"All right."

"No, really Dirt. This is killer."

"OK, that's enough." Dirt began to feel uncomfortable. "I don't like doing nice stuff, so knock it off. It's not that big a deal anyway. I really only had to buy the bag and the putter and those are both used. The rest of the clubs are all just clubs these idiots left behind and never came back for."

Donnie noticed that he didn't have a matching set, but it didn't matter.

"That's a pretty good driver in there," Dirt told him. "You'll need to get your own golf balls. All the ones we use here are crap driving range balls that don't fly worth a crap."

"Thanks a lot. I mean it, Dirt." Donnie stood and approached Dirt.

"Hold it, right there," Dirt said. "You're not going to hug me, are you?"

"No." Donnie wasn't sure why he stood. He only knew that he wanted to show his gratitude.

"Men shake hands, Donnie," Dirt explained. "On something like this, you shake a man's hand. You should have shaken my hand when I offered you the job, too."

"Why didn't you shake mine?"

"Hey! Every guy likes a girl's ass but no guy likes a smart-ass!"

He put his hand out. Donnie took it.

"That's not a handshake," Dirt exclaimed.

"What?"

"Put some mustard behind it. Nice and tight. Let me know you're there. Come on. Try again."

They shook hands again. "That's it," Dirt said. "Squeeze a little harder. There you go. That's a handshake."

Megan pulled into the gravel lot.

"Seen her before," Dirt said. "That your girlfriend?"

"Yeah."

Dirt's face registered mild shock. "You do all right, Donnie."

"You bet." He threw the bag over his shoulder. "Thanks again for the clubs."

"Get out of here."

Donnie's feet crunched across the gravel and he got into the van with Megan.

They drove for nearly an hour and got lost on a bunch of farm roads. Donnie reassured her that as long as they had a map in the van, he would be able to get them back. They parked in an open field and got out.

Megan had wisely stopped at the storage unit to pick up one of their Haviland Platypus blankets that they used to get through the winter. Donnie whipped the blanket open and they lounged out on it.

"So, Dirt gave you those clubs as a gift?" Megan asked.

"Yup."

"For what?"

"Don't really know."

"That's cool. Don't let my dad see them. He's pissed that you didn't have any and missed that tournament."

Donnie laughed.

Megan took out her newly purchased astronomy book. It was the first time she opened it and had a hard time making anything out. She handed it to Donnie for his assistance. Donnie looked back and forth from the sky to the book, but couldn't decipher any more than the two constellations that everyone knew – the big dipper and the little dipper.

"Forget this," he said and tossed the book aside.

"Hey! I paid twenty bucks for that."

"It's not doing us any good." He laid back and put his hands behind his head.

She crawled over him to retrieve the book. Then, with his body underneath her, she changed her mind and snuggled up to him. "Mmmm," she moaned and gave him a kiss. "You're yummy."

Her single kiss led to an onslaught of more kisses. Alone, in the open field and reclined on the blanket, they found new ways to fool around. Hands slipped under shirts and down into pants. Each new touch was arousing in an unfamiliar way. She kissed his neck; he kissed her belly. At no time did they invade undergarments, even though the thought had crossed their minds.

When they were done exploring each other enough for one night, they settled back on the blanket and gazed at the night sky.

"Look how beautiful it is," Megan said. Both kids were flat on their backs, hands held, fingers intertwined. "You forget what it's like. Look how the horizon is black, you know? It doesn't have that glow. We have to come out here every month so we don't forget."

Donnie looked at the stars in space. "Makes me feel small. Insignificant."

"Not to me, you're not."

"But overall… if we didn't have each other, what would there be? We're just one small planet rotating around a dying star. We're just one small solar system in just one galaxy out of thousands, maybe more? We're just a grain of sand."

As they had done so often in the past, they kept each other company in silence. Their bodies relaxed. Their faces softened. Their bones became heavy, and together, they melted into the Earth.

Megan stared at the quarter moon for a long time before she asked, "Do you suppose the moon wishes that it were the sun?"

"I'm sure it's happy with being the moon."

"But its only light is what it reflects."

"That's important, though."

She rolled toward him. "I bet it wishes it was a star."

"I bet that it's content with revolving around the Earth." He kissed her on the forehead. "I know I am."

She closed her eyes. "This is comfortable. You know, being able to lie down? We should get a mattress for Unit #143."

"Yeah. It'd be a comfortable option, that's for sure."

"Yeah."

Everything was so tranquil that they dozed off.

A little later, Donnie woke and nudged Megan. "What time is it?" he asked her.

She felt groggy and didn't want to get up from the comfort of his body but managed to drag herself to the van. She turned the key halfway until the digital clock turned on.

"Holy shit!" She screamed, now wide awake. "It's almost four!"

Donnie jumped up, grabbing the blanket, book, and light. Later he would feel bad about leaving their empty soda cans behind, but in the moment, he knew they had to get a move on.

T W E N T Y

Donnie was accurate in proclaiming that he would be able to get them home with the use of a map. Problems arose when they discovered that the van did not have a map in it.

It took over half an hour of driving around to figure out where they were. Once they did, Donnie informed Megan that they were even farther away from home than where they were when they fell asleep.

"Oh, that's just great," she responded.

"Are you in trouble?"

"I imagine so."

"Slow down."

Megan was speeding along the vacant roads.

"Easy for you to say," she said. "Your mom is at work."

"Yeah, but I'll tell her anyway."

"Why?"

"It was an accident. We didn't mean to come home this late. She'll understand." Or not care, he thought.

"Bizarre."

They pulled into Megan's driveway a little after 6:00 A.M. The lights were on inside her house.

Her tone was calm and even, "I'm so dead."

"See you tomorrow?"

"I seriously doubt you'll see me before school on Monday."

Donnie smiled. For some reason, it was humorous to him. "Good luck."

"It's not funny."

"Right." He got out of the car.

She pulled into the garage.

Her father was eating a bowl of cereal at the kitchen table and her mother had a cup of coffee in front of her.

Megan set the car keys down on the table. "I'm sorry."

Her father stood and when he did, he became a very intimidating man. "Explain where you have been," he demanded.

"I was out with Donnie. We lost track of time…"

"Lost track of time! How do you lose track of time seven hours past curfew? Explain that to me!"

"We just did."

Her mother's voice was tender yet stern, "We've been worrying about you. We didn't know where you were or what you were doing…"

Her father interrupted, "Exactly what were you doing? You aren't just a few minutes late. You're several hours late!"

"Donnie… He… We were…" She didn't know what to say or how to explain. Stumbling over her words made her appear guilty even though she committed no crime other than being out past curfew.

"Come here! I want to smell your breath."

"Dad…"

"*Come'ere!*"

She walked directly to him and breathed on his face. The scent of alcohol was absent. Taking hold of her chin, he forced her head up so he could look into her eyes.

"Why are your eyes red?" he wanted to know.

"She's probably tired," Megan's mom offered.

"I'm really sorry…" Megan just wanted it to be over. She wanted to go to bed and wake up to a new day. Everything was perfect just a few hours ago. The clear night sky, the quarter moon, Donnie – everything. Her dad was ruining it. He was making her feel like a teenager again.

"When you left the house with our car, where did you go?"

She had never seen him so angry; furthermore, this was the most dialogue she had had with him in weeks, which made it depressing.

"I took the van…" Megan was trying not to cry.

"I know that part! I want to know every detail. Tell me step by step where you've been and what you did!"

"I don't know." Her solitary tear didn't soften her father's attitude one bit.

"Think!"

"OK, ok, ok… I picked up Donnie at the driving range. He put his clubs in the van…"

"I thought you told me that he didn't have clubs!"

Megan whimpered, "He didn't. He just got them. Today… er, yesterday… Dirt gave them to him as a gift."

"Who?"

"Dirt. He owns the driving range."

"I didn't see Donnie with them when he got out of the van."

She spoke as if she were pleading for her life, "They're still in the van."

Her father breathed heavily in and out of his nose. "Empty your pockets."

"There's nothing in them," she sobbed.

"Where's your purse?"

"She doesn't have one," her mother told him.

"Where do you keep your license?" he barked.

Megan held up her wallet.

"Empty it," he ordered. "Empty everything out of your pocketbook on the table."

Her voice was nearly inaudible, "Dad, there's nothing…"

His face formed an angry frown that prompted Megan to quickly empty its contents. No suspicious materials were found.

"Pick up that phone. Call Donnie. Tell him to be here in one hour. We're going golfing!"

"But dad…"

He slammed his hand down flat on the table. It rattled and the contents of Megan's purse bounced everywhere. "Do it!"

Timidly, she retrieved the cordless phone from its receiver and began punching in Donnie's phone number.

Megan's mom said to her father, "Let's get her a cell phone…"

"Nonsense!" he disagreed. "I will not give her a cell phone so she can yak on it all day and arrange secret rendezvous with her friends. She needs to learn and exercise good ol' fashioned responsibility first and foremost."

Donnie answered the phone. He greeted her with a sleepy, "Hello," and a yawn. He had already fallen asleep. Megan was jealous.

"Donnie?" Megan mumbled, trying to compose herself the best she could.

"Who else would it be?" he said. He was, after all, the only guy who lived in the house.

She wiped the tears away and tried hard to steady her voice. "My dad would like to play a round of golf with you."

The cobwebs were beginning to clear from his head. "Oh geez, the golf clubs. I left them in your car."

"Yeah."

"Sure, I guess I have to."

"Yeah. Um," she turned away from her parents, "he'd like for you to come over in an hour."

"To golf?"

"Yeah."

"That doesn't sound good."

"It's not."

"Tell him I have to work."

She turned around to pass the message on to her father. His hardened mug showed that no excuse would be acceptable.

"No," Megan said. "I think you better come over in an hour."

Donnie exhaled and collapsed back on his bed. "All right."

TWENTY-ONE

Every student in Haviland High dreaded that first day back to school until they got there. It was a giant reunion and a new start for those looking for a better school year than the last. They got to explore new classrooms and subjects with different teachers and students. Everyone was happy to see all of their friends and how they had or hadn't changed over the summer.

Mr. Priddy wanted to ground Megan until Christmas, but her mom intervened and she received a lenient ten days instead. During her grounding, Megan was not permitted to use the television, stereo, or computer. She almost wished for homework on that first day just so she had something to do. As part of her grounding, she was not permitted to walk to or from school. Her mother drove her both ways.

That prevented her from seeing Donnie until third period. They were in the same Chemistry class. It was the first chance they got to talk about the weekend's fiasco.

"What did my dad do to you?" Megan asked.

"What did he tell you?" All weekend long, he watched the Priddy house for signs of life. He was interested to know what was going on inside of it.

"He didn't say anything about it. He's hardly spoken to me at all. Well? Did you guys really go golfing? What happened out there?"

"I'm a crappy putter."

"Donnie!" She puffed. "I mean with my dad."

"He was pretty good except for the par three, seventh. I birdied. He like bogeyed or double bogeyed."

Megan stared at him with a blank expression, her mini-version of the silent treatment.

Donnie gave up his act of suspense. "I don't really know what happened. I mean... He paid for me to play a round of golf on his fancy-pants course so we could discuss 'business'."

"'Business'?"

"Yeah. You're probably unaware of it, but your dad and I have several business transactions pending. Afterwards, we discussed them with the boys over scotch and cigars."

"Really?"

"No, not really. When did you get so gullible? You must be going stir crazy over there."

"You have no idea."

Donnie slid his backpack off. "He talked about your sister for some reason or another and then he made an analogy to me being a predator... I'm not sure. I think that he wanted to sound threatening, but it was more confusing than anything."

"What does Kara have to do with it? Why was he talking about her?"

"He never really said. After I sank my sand shot on the seventh, he was in an even worse mood than when we started."

Megan greeted one of her friends who sat down on the other side of her. When she was done, she informed Donnie that she was under house arrest.

"For ten days," he replied.

"He told you?"

"Yup."

"I've also lost driving privileges indefinitely." That was Megan's mom's compromise with her dad for the shortened sentence.

The late bell rang and they sat down next to each other. Five minutes later, the teacher handed out assigned seats and they were two rows apart.

After class, they reunited. Both of them were headed to study hall. They compared schedules to see if they shared any other classes after that, but they did not. Two was better than zero and zero was how many they shared the previous year.

On their way down the hall, Donnie showed her a notebook. The black cover was crinkled with white creases and the corners were tattered. "This one here…," he said before losing his voice. It was the first time he held that notebook in quite a while. "I… um, I know that you must be bored over there so… And I didn't want you to forget me… This notebook…" He pulled her aside and waited for the foot traffic to die down. "This is the notebook I was using when my dad…" Then he couldn't say it. He thought that he would be able to detach himself from the tragedy long enough to get it out, but he struggled. The weight of the notebook was too much.

Donnie leveled his eyes at Megan. Her soft face was inviting. Reflected in it was the sorrow that he felt but not the helplessness. Megan knew that she didn't fully understand his misfortunes, but that wasn't going to keep her from listening and waiting to see how she could be what he needed. Donnie's stoic toughness began to give. His lips started to quiver. He missed having a father.

"It's all right," Megan said with eyes that were ready to cry on his behalf. "I get it."

Donnie swallowed. "This is the first notebook," he explained. "It's me. How I felt. Who I am. I don't read it. I don't even open it. But… I thought that you…"

"I'd love to read it."

He began to ramble. "I don't know what's in it or if it's any good or if it makes sense…"

"Donnie, it doesn't matter." She tried to keep the conversation light. "Hey, I'm grounded. Like you said, I'm bored out of my mind. I'll read anything."

He nodded, "Yeah, OK," and reluctantly relinquished the notebook.

Megan immediately slipped it into her satchel. She lightly touched his forearm. They were late for study hall.

During lunch on that first day back, friends reunited and discussed the summer's developments. They also immediately started putting together plans for weekend activities.

"We should all go to the movies Friday," Sada announced to her table.

"Absolutely," Alyssa, the outcast cheerleader agreed. The only reason she was on the squad was because she was tiny and easy to toss into the air. "But we also need to go somewhere where there'll be fun."

"You mean boys?" Megan said.

"Boys. Fun. Fun. Boys," Alyssa said. "It's all the same thing. I know the football team will be bowling at Ubu Lanes on Friday."

"The football team?" Sada said without hiding any disgust. "Gag."

"C'mon. Admit it. Some of them are at least fun to look at."

"A few," Sada conceded. "What's Donnie doing on Friday, Megan? Let's hang out with him and a few of his friends. A summer tan worked wonders for that boy."

"I can't go," Megan said.

"Why not?"

"I'm sentenced to ten days of house arrest."

"No way!" Alyssa said.

It was the first time that Megan had ever been grounded and the other seven girls at the table wanted to know what offense she committed to land herself in the halfway house.

"What did you do?" Sada asked, when Megan didn't immediately offer it up.

It didn't feel right taking their relationship public, but now that school was back in session, it would become nearly impossible to keep it a secret. "I was making out with Donnie Betts, fell asleep, and didn't get home until like six in the morning."

It was fresh ink for the high school tabloids. Every girl stared at her, dumbfounded. Then, simultaneously, all of them looked a few tables down to Donnie.

Dale, still with his cheesy mustache, never missed something like this. "That whole table of girls just looked at us."

Donnie glanced over his shoulder. Every girl there diligently resumed eating their lunch.

"They all just looked away when you looked," Dale said, worried that Donnie wouldn't believe him. "Who do you think they're looking at?"

Donnie shrugged and opened his carton of milk.

Dale leaned back on the hind two legs of his chair and examined them. "Hey, some of them are looking pretty good. Sada's wearing less black make-up, Alyssa perked up, you know?... Everyone over there is looking a little hotter... 'Cept Priddy, she got a little thicker in the thighs. Too much Friendly's for that chick."

Dale's comment caught Donnie on a day when his emotions were floating close to the surface. It reminded him too much of the guilt, embarrassment, and disgrace that he felt with his dad's suicide. Shame burst out of Donnie like steam through the layer of skin on boiling milk. He turned angry at his father for being a coward instead of a hero.

Donnie made two movements and they were both swift. He was holding his milk in his right hand. He half dumped, half tossed it on Dale. Dale's chair began tilting back down to all four legs. With the same hand that held the milk, Donnie made a fist, reached out with his long arm, and popped him in the mouth.

Dale's chair fell over backwards and he crashed to the floor. He didn't get up. There was no fight.

Everyone stopped and looked. No one would have guessed that it was Donnie Betts who laid him out. And no one knew how to react because it was Donnie Betts.

The only movement in the cafeteria was the slow tears that trickled down Donnie's cheeks.

TWENTY-TWO

With Megan grounded and Donnie suspended from school for fighting, they didn't get to see each other for the rest of the week. Even though Megan was the one who had the benefit of interaction with the other kids at school, she was the one who felt lonely.

Donnie enjoyed his solitude. He valued time away from school. He hadn't mentally prepared for that first day back and he needed to regroup and collect his thoughts. It wasn't like him to let his emotions get the best of him and create a scene. If Megan wasn't grounded, he would have felt bad for missing out on time with her at Unit #143. As it were, all he was missing out on was school, and he didn't miss it much.

Getting confused from having so many days off, Donnie went to the driving range at ten o'clock Friday morning instead of Saturday.

He was greeted by Dirt and his ear hair with a curt, "What are you doing here?"

Donnie stopped walking and looked at Dirt as if he were the crazy one.

"Didn't school start?" Dirt asked.

"Yeah," Donnie answered. "What day is it?"

"Friday, kid! You better get on over to Haviland High."

Donnie pulled the baseball helmet down over his Pirate's hat and picked up his scoop. "I've been suspended."

"Suspended?" Dirt was skeptical. Donnie didn't seem capable of being suspended. "What did you do?"

"Fighting."

"You don't look beat up."

"There was only one punch."

"You knocked him out?"

"Down for the count." Donnie wasn't bragging, just conveying what had happened.

"You're taller in inches than you are heavy in pounds. Who were you fighting? Elmo?"

Donnie shrugged.

Dirt smiled. "He said something about that girl of yours, didn't he?"

When Donnie didn't reply, Dirt laughed and walked to the recesses of the shack. Donnie went out to collect golf balls.

Megan missed Donnie. Between her house arrest and his suspension, she never got to see him, talk to him, or hang out with him. Instead of making it easier on her, reading Donnie's personal entries in his makeshift journal made her long for him even more. She could have read the entire thing in one night, but refrained. She wanted to make it last the entire week.

Donnie delved into subject matters that she had never pondered. There were several instances when she felt the pain he described and wanted to give him a hug. His darker thoughts would have creeped her out had she not gotten to know him so well before reading it. Donnie seemed to be searching for the perfect hero, the perfect role model, some grand figure that constantly eluded him.

Some of the material still managed to scare her. One page was a handwritten copy of Hamlet's "To Be or Not to Be" soliloquy. Until reading it in Donnie's notebook, she hadn't realized that Hamlet was contemplating suicide. For the first time, she understood that Donnie had considered following in his father's footsteps. What would life in Haviland had been like for her if Donnie was gone before she even arrived?

When she met him, he didn't stick out as a troubled youth. She now saw through his awkward charm and shy behavior. Donnie was a survivor. He had developed a unique emotional strength to endure the troubles he faced. He was more experienced in life than any of his peers and that made him more mature. Donnie was a well-adjusted youth when he could have turned out to be a total wreck. Megan admired him.

Friday night, when all of her friends were going to the bowling alley and the movies, Megan Priddy finished reading Donnie's black notebook. She placed it in the drawer of her white night stand and pushed it shut. Before she fell asleep, she began to dream of her boyfriend. Waiting until Monday to see him again seemed like an eternity.

She dozed off after satisfying herself with pleasurable thoughts of him.

The next morning she woke up with a plan. Waiting until her father left for golf and her mother went outside to plant chrysanthemums, Megan used the purple phone in her room to quickly put a call in to Donnie.

He was lying flat on his back in bed, listening to the all alternative rock station on his clock/radio. Before Megan and the storage unit, he seldom listened to music. After being away from it for a week, he was beginning to miss it and tuned in to one of their favorite stations. When the phone rang, he had no desire to get out of bed to answer it, but since his mother was sleeping after working all night, he jumped up and ran down the hall to pick it up.

"Donnie?" Megan used a whisper just in case she had misjudged where her parents were.

"Megan?"

"Yeah. Listen. Watch for my parents to leave tonight for their weekly date. After they've gone, head over to Unit #143. I'm going to wait around for a little in case they call, after they do, I'll sneak over for a little bit."

"Are you sure?" Donnie didn't like the idea of taking this risk when it would be less than a week until Megan would be allowed to leave the house again.

Megan thought of the black notebook, the touch of Donnie's hands against her body, and the feel of his lips against hers. "Hell yeah, I'm sure."

He wanted to see her just as bad and didn't argue any more than he already had. "See you there."

Later that night, he waited for the Priddys' headlights to vanish down the street and he began his trek to Parkside Storage.

Donnie never wore a watch and Unit #143 didn't have a clock. Foolishly, he didn't bring anything to write on or to read. He played solitaire for a while, but became bored. He began to think that Megan had bagged the idea of meeting him. Maybe she decided that it wasn't worth the risk or maybe when her parents called, they said they would be home soon and she didn't have enough time to sneak out.

After an undeterminable amount of time, Donnie allowed himself to feel disappointed that Megan wasn't coming. He hadn't anticipated seeing her until Monday at school, but all day long, the excitement of meeting with her earlier than that had been building. Now all he had was the chalk outline of her. There she was – a perfect outline of her body. He could picture her standing there. Donnie thought of the previous Saturday when they were alone in the field and fell asleep looking at the stars. Both left wanting more. Donnie's imagination put forth scenarios that aroused him.

Since he was alone, Donnie decided to do something that always ended with an intense moment of pleasure and incredible relaxation. He pulled his jeans and underwear down around his ankles. Observing the chalk outline of his girlfriend and recalling all the sensations of the previous Saturday with her, Donnie drifted into an unconscious focus as he mindlessly stroked himself.   He was in no hurry. Getting there was half the fun.

The door flung up with Megan saying, "Sorry it took so long for… Whoa."

Donnie blew out the candles on the card table before he did anything else. This way when he pulled up his jeans, he would be hidden in the shadows.

"Hold it just a sec," she told him before he had the jeans past his knees.

Megan had a pretty good idea of what was going on in the storage unit when she arrived. She would have thought that something like that would have grossed her out, but it really wasn't that big of a deal. All boys did it, didn't they? At least most of them. Maybe even some girls.

"Um, Megan…," Donnie tried to sound casual, but he couldn't pull it off. He didn't like waiting around for her permission to finish getting dressed.

"Don't be embarrassed or anything like that," Megan told him. "I'm not going to make fun of you. It's a natural thing, I think." She was curious. She wanted to ask him all kinds of questions about it, but simplified it into one, "Were you thinking of me?"

Donnie cleared his throat. "Yeah, I was. OK?"

"Oh, Donnie. I'm flattered."

"Great. Can I pull my pants up now?"

"K," she said. "But from now on, that's your chair."

TWENTY-THREE

The Wednesday after Donnie was caught doing his thing in the storage unit, Megan was released from the halfway house. The time between lunch and the final bell seemed abnormally long. They couldn't wait to walk to Unit #143 after school.

Duplicating the routine from their sophomore year, Donnie stopped at Swifts for drinks and snacks while Megan went on ahead to start her homework.

When Donnie showed up, Megan played on the incident of that weekend by asking, "Can you find a way to entertain yourself until I'm done?"

His face registered disapproval of her joke, but she knew that he wasn't upset by it. He removed a thin book from his backpack and read.

Megan took nearly an hour of frustrations out on her pen cap until she completed her math homework. She slammed her book closed and asked Donnie what he was reading.

"*Jonathan Livingston Seagull*," he replied.

"For school?" Megan had the same literature teacher as Donnie and temporarily became nervous that she had missed an assignment.

"No."

"Don't tell me it's about seagulls."

"I won't."

"Well, is it?"

"Yup."

"What's with you and books about animals?"

Donnie grinned at her rhetorical question.

"Is it good?" she asked.

"Yup."

"Will you read it out loud to me?" Megan had gotten used to listening to audio books that summer.

"Nope."

"It looks short," she said, trying to change his mind.

"Yeah." He had nearly finished it while waiting for her to complete her homework. "It wouldn't take you long to read on your own."

"What does he do?"

"Who?"

"Jonathan."

Donnie considered this for a moment. He read simply for the enjoyment of it. He seldom analyzed what he was reading so it took him a good thirty seconds to come up with something. "He doesn't accept being like the other seagulls. They're happy with just flying around for food. Jonathan is about becoming better at flying. He practices all the time. He's sort of a hero except the flock eventually banishes him because they don't get it."

Megan took the book from his hands. She looked at the cover and examined a few of the photographs inside. "How's he a hero, then, if no one wants him around?"

Donnie never sounded surer of himself. "Because he strives to achieve something more out of life even when others find his ambition threatening. He presses on even though his choice isn't popular. He doesn't give in. He's *more* of a hero because he's not admired by those around him."

She twirled some of her peachy hair around a finger. "That's some seagull."

He tossed the book in his backpack. "Yeah."

"Double solitaire?"

"Sure."

They each shuffled a deck of cards and dealt.

"Hold on a sec," Donnie said. He walked over to turn up the radio. "I dig this song."

"Really?" It was Donnie's active interest in music that surprised Megan, not that he liked a particular song. He had never turned up the radio before.

"Yeah. There's just those two guitar chords that bounce back and forth until they get to the chorus and then they add a third."

Megan stopped mid-game and looked at him.

Donnie didn't take notice. "The lyrics are kind of cool, too." He looked over at her cards. "If you play that three of clubs, I can play my four."

"Since when did you become a music connoisseur?" Megan wanted to know.

"Since you started making me listen to the radio non-stop."

"Forget this." Megan scrambled the cards up on the table. She grabbed Donnie's tambourine and rattled it. "Let's rock!" She beat the instrument to the bass drum of the song and danced, wiggling her butt to the ground and back up.

Donnie jumped up, flung his front leg forward, swung it behind him, spun around, and went into a disco groove.

When the song was over and they settled back down, Donnie and Megan watched the sun set behind the row of storage units across from theirs.

The sun created unique colors as it came closer to the horizon.

"Funny, how it looks like the sun is setting when really it's us rotating," Donnie said.

"I never really thought about it. You're right." She reached out and took his hand. "Look how cool the sky is over there."

Donnie followed her eyes to a point in the sky where the lowering sun shot rays of light through a thin grouping of clouds. Against the darkening blue skies, those clouds were an iridescent, fiery pink.

"That's far out," he agreed.

They watched without saying anything until the sun was gone, the sky was dark, and it was time to walk home.

Megan had to work from six until close on the first Saturday in September. Donnie knocked off work a little after four to meet her at Unit #143 for an hour or so before her shift started.

"Happy birthday!" Megan said when he pulled the door up. She wore her Friendly's uniform and her hair swung side-to-side in a ponytail.

Donnie set his backpack down on a chair and walked over to her. He spoke in a low voice as if he were trying to keep from embarrassing her in front of a large crowd even though the two of them were alone in the storage unit. "My birthday's not until next month."

She whispered back, "I know," and winked.

"Then why'd you get me a gift?"

"Who said anything about a gift?"

"It's giant," Donnie said pointing to the large gift-wrapped item in her hand. "It's nearly as big as you."

"You're right. This is your birthday gift."

"Why's it in Christmas wrapping paper?"

"All I had."

Donnie took a root beer from the cooler.

"My mom dragged me to some charity flea market on Sunday," Megan explained. "I saw this and thought of you. Why wait until the end of October for your birthday? I figure, give it to you now so you can start using it." She held it out in front of her, "Guess what it is."

With the gift wrap tightly wrapped around it, it was obviously shaped like a guitar.

Donnie shook his head back and forth, "No idea."

Megan tilted her head to one side. "I think you're lying."

"Well, I might have one guess."

"Go for it."

"A blender."

"Close!" She thrust it against his chest. "Open it and see."

Donnie ripped off the holiday paper and, sure enough, it was an acoustic guitar.

"How groovalicious is that?" Megan said.

"I don't know how to play guitar."

"No shit. How could you if you never owned one?"

He looked it over. He didn't know the first thing about guitars, but it looked to be in good condition. There was only one problem. "No strings?" he asked.

From the back pocket of her black work pants, she whipped out a small package of strings and tossed it at him. "I've got a guitar pick in my other back pocket, but I'll let you get that out yourself."

Donnie pulled the garage door down. He turned around to face her.

Her smile was mischievous. "I believe, Donnie, that it is at the very bottom of my pocket. You'll have to dig deep for it."

TWENTY-FOUR

Leaves were falling and it was too chilly to go outside without a jacket.

Inside Unit #143, Donnie sat with his guitar. It took him a week or two just to figure out how to properly tune it, but once he did, he immediately began to learn the basics. He was concerned that his practicing disturbed Megan's studying.

"I like listening to you play," she'd tell him.

"It's hardly playing."

"You're learning. I can tell that you're improving."

He'd continue to make odd twangy noises with his instrument while Megan went on studying.

She was right, though. His playing had improved. Donnie could pick a string of notes to a familiar tune and he had a half dozen chords mastered. They spent a lot of time in the storage unit and Donnie played a little every time they were there. He wasn't to the point where he could play a whole song, but it wouldn't be long.

Megan sat with the Sunday ads spread out in front of her. Her goal was to find a mattress they could afford.

The chairs that came with the card table were still good for homework and playing cards, but they were no longer comfortable for extended hours of use. A mattress would be good for reading or sleeping. It could be used to rest on before or after a work shift. It would serve as a couch when they listened to audio books. A mattress would be much more relaxing than slouching in the chairs for most of their storage unit activities.

They looked forward to lounging on it together. Hugs were nice, but not possible to sustain for a long time if they were standing or sitting. On the bed, though, they could hold each other forever. Donnie and Megan wanted to be able to replicate their positions on the night they took the fieldtrip to stargaze.

"Here's the one we want," Megan said, tapping down on an ad. "It's on sale."

"Where is it?" Donnie asked without looking up from the positioning of his fingers on the guitar.

"Some store near the mall. The price is boffo and I bet it's so comfortable. Look at it," she held up the ad.

It just looked like another mattress to Donnie. "Sure." He leaned his guitar against the wall and turned on the radio. He asked, "Megan, when we get it, do you think that we'll… you know?"

"What's 'you know'?"

"You know what 'you know' is."

She played dumb. "I don't know what you're talking about, Donnie Betts."

"You know."

"Eat ice cream on it?"

"No."

"Jump up and down on it?"

"No."

"Lean it against the wall and crawl underneath like we're camping."

"No. You know."

Megan shrugged her shoulders, shook her head, and said with the slightest grin sneaking through, "Sorry, Donnie, don't know what you're talking about."

Donnie knew that she knew but just wanted to hear him say it. He gave in and spoke the one word, "Sex."

"Ohhhhhh. That 'you know'."

"Yeah, that 'you know.' Now you know, so now you have to answer my question."

Megan thought that all high school boys wanted to "you know" and it wasn't any secret that Donnie liked her big time. So, if he was crushing on her in a major way and a high school boy, it was logical to conclude that he wanted to "you know" with her. She was pretty sure of it.

Megan had an answer to his question but wanted to leave the window open just in case she changed her mind, so she offered him a "Maybe."

Donnie went back to his guitar.

"K," Megan said, looking again at the advertisement. "The sale ends Saturday. How are we going to get it?"

"We can't. You're not allowed to drive." A mattress wouldn't fit in Donnie's car. They needed Megan's mini-van.

"But the sale is going to end."

"So what? We'd have enough for it even if it wasn't on sale."

"I don't want to wait. Do you?"

"No, but what're we gonna do? Hijack your family's van?"

Her face lit up. She rushed to the opposite side of the table and gave Donnie a big smooch on the cheek. "That's a wonderful idea! I'll wait until they go out Saturday night and take the van to get it."

"That's a horrible idea."

"Do you always follow all the rules, Donnie?"

"If you get caught, how are you going to explain a mattress in your car? There's gotta be another way."

"K," she said, her lips curving up at the corners. She placed her hands on her hips. "I want this mattress here by the end of the week. If you can come up with another way, then we'll do that. If not, I'm hijacking the van. And don't tell me that it can wait because it can't."

"What do you mean, 'it can't'?"

"It just can't."

"Fine." Donnie was unruffled. "We'll have it delivered."

She mimicked his lazy reply, "Fine, we'll have it delivered." She put her arms through the sleeves of her coat. "Fine, let's go get your car."

Along with the new mattress, Megan insisted that they buy sheets with a very high thread count. The only way Donnie could tell the difference between the high thread count sheets and the lower ones was by the price. Higher was high.

Donnie told her, "I don't even care if we have sheets."

Megan wrinkled her nose. "Nasty."

"How are we going to wash them anyway?"

"We'll worry about that later. Let's look at comforters."

"But we got those Haviland High blankets. What's wrong with those?"

They compromised. Instead of a comforter, they agreed on using the blankets they already had and purchased sheets that were on the more expensive side.

The sales clerk's hair was not its natural color. It was store bought and she had done it herself. She may have thought that it assisted her in aging gracefully, but it only made it more apparent that she was aging. She had worked at the furniture store over sixteen years and her only concern was her next sales commission. She didn't care that the address Megan provided her was for a storage facility.

She said with a southern accent, "We can deliver it on Monday between noon and three."

Donnie and Megan looked at each other. They knew exactly what the other was thinking – school. Both turned back to face the sales clerk.

"Do you deliver on the weekends?" Donnie asked.

"Saturdays. But that's a popular day for deliveries," she told them, chomping on a stick of gum. With fingernails as fake as the color of her hair, she pecked at the keyboard. "The earliest Saturday opening we have is four weeks."

Donnie and Megan communicated again just by looking at each other. This time their faces recognized disagreement.

Donnie spoke first, "If we buy it today, can you hold it for us for a couple of weeks until we get a chance to pick it up instead of having it delivered?" There was no way they could fit the mattress and box spring in Donnie's car. In two or three weeks, Megan would have her driving privileges reinstated and they would be able to pick it up without a delivery fee and without missing school.

The sales clerk began to answer, "The reason this model is on sale…"

Megan cut her off, "Monday is fine."

Later in the car, Donnie wanted to know, "Monday between noon and three? How's that going to work?"

Megan's reply was a simple statement of the obvious, "One of us will have to skip school."

"One of us? How about: you have to skip school on Monday. I'm not the one who agreed to being there."

"Since when was school so important to you?"

"What if I don't want to?" he said, looking at her.

"Instead of skipping then, you can knock out another one of your friends and get suspended again."

"Ha ha."

Donnie's eyes went back to the road and when they did, he saw the stopped car that they were rapidly approaching for the first time. He sucked in a quick breath of air and held it. Megan let out a scream. If he had had time to contemplate what was happening, he most certainly would have panicked; however, it happened so fast, he didn't get the chance.

Donnie's right foot smashed down on the brake pedal. All four tires shrieked in pain as they left a black trail of tire blood on the road. A moment before impact, Donnie knew that they wouldn't stop in time. The opposite side of the road was filled with oncoming traffic. Simultaneously, Donnie released his foot off the break and turned the wheel to the right. The car swerved quickly around thc stalled car and bounced down off the pavement. Gravel, grass, and discarded trash spit up from the berm and ricocheted off the car. Donnie and Megan were jostled from side to side and bumped up and down. Donnie pulled the wheel back to the left and they were on the road again, traveling as if nothing happened.

Both exhaled for the first time since recognizing the stopped vehicle on the road.

Donnie ignored his fluttering heart and asked Megan, "Are you OK?"

"I think I peed my pants."

"Yeah, me too."

"No. Seriously. I think I peed my pants."

TWENTY-FIVE

Donnie pulled the car into Friendly's parking lot. Megan went straight to the restroom while he got a booth in the back, near the kitchen and servers' station.

In the safety of a restroom stall, Megan examined her underwear and jeans. Her hope was that she was imagining it. The jeans were mostly dry, but the purple undies were wet. She removed her shoes, then her jeans. She slid her underwear down and off. A wave of embarrassment flowed through her and she instinctively hid her face in her hands. She smelled urine and immediately knew why. She was still holding her underwear.

"Nasty!" she screamed and dropped them.

She laughed at herself and the embarrassment passed. On her way out but prior to washing up, she threw away her soiled underwear.

She slid into the seat across from Donnie and picked up a menu. She knew everything that was on it, but needed something to occupy her hands.

"Well?" Donnie smiled. "Did you?"

"You should pay more attention when you're driving!"

He laughed.

"What is it," she said, "that causes people to lose control of their bladder when they're frightened?"

"Why are you asking me? You're the expert."

Each ordered a cheeseburger with fries and a milkshake. They were going to split a single shake, but Donnie wanted chocolate and Megan wanted strawberry.

Megan used her employee discount and paid for their meals.

On the way to Unit #143 Megan said, "I have to quit that place. The food there is making me fat again."

"I think you look good, but if you want, I can see if Dirt needs someone to work the shack with him."

Megan shuddered at the thought of being stuck in the shack with Dirt. "No, thanks."

Donnie parked the car in front of their storage unit and they got out.

"Actually," Megan said, "I'm going to quit without getting another job."

"Yeah, right," Donnie said. He removed the lock and pulled the door open. "We'd run out of money and have to give up the storage unit."

She pulled the door closed behind them. Donnie began lighting the candles. Megan usually turned on the radio next. This time she did not.

Megan took Donnie's hands. "There's something I need to tell you." Dread dripped from her words. "We just found out for sure Friday."

Donnie was confused. Megan sounded serious. Who was "we"? Was she going to break up with him? Was that why she didn't need the job anymore – because they would no longer be sharing the storage unit? That couldn't be. They just purchased the bed. How could he have been so foolish? Megan had found someone else. She was purchasing the bed to… To what? Where would she keep it if not in the storage unit? It wasn't making sense. He asked, "We?…"

"My family," Megan told him.

"What are you talking about?"

"My, um… My dad got a…" Megan noticed that she was staring at Donnie's chest. She forced herself to make eye contact. "He got a promotion, sort of. He's going to a different division… more money…"

Donnie didn't understand why that was bad news.

Megan explained, "We have to move again."

"Far?"

"Pittsburgh."

"Pittsburgh?"

"Yeah, you know," she said, forcing a smile and tugging on his hat, "the Pirates."

Donnie felt a chasm open inside his chest. His body and energy were sucked through the black hole at its bottom.

He began to vanish before Megan's eyes. Everything external about him began to turn outside in. He was running from the world and finding solace within himself. She wrapped her arms around him and held him close. Her touch. Her arms around him and her body pressed against his was what kept Donnie in the present moment.

She, not Donnie, was the one who began to cry. "That's why we couldn't wait on getting the mattress," she said. "I'll be gone in less than a month."

Donnie's voice sounded like a spirit had taken over his body and was speaking through him, "A month?"

"Probably less. My mom is already looking for a house up there. There's going to be snow in the winter. How crazy will that be?" Her attempt at conversation failed. Donnie was not in the mood to discuss the quirks of her new city. "So that's why I wanted to get the mattress right away. I want us to make the most of our time together."

"How could you…?" his words trailed off. He said them again. His lips barely moved. The words were nearly inaudible, "How could you…?" He pried his body away from her.

"Donnie, stop," she protested.

He took off his Pirates hat and flung it across the unit. It hit the wall and fell limply to the ground. On his way out, he scooped up his guitar.

"Donnie. Please, don't…," Megan pleaded.

The garage door rattled up and clanged at the top. He got in the car and drove off.

Megan was left alone in the storage unit. She had lots of tears but no tissues. As she watched him drive away, she quietly said to herself, "Walking is much safer than riding with you, anyhow," but without her boyfriend around to hear it, the joke just saddened her more.

———————

The next morning, Megan Priddy looked back down her street to Donnie's home. She waited at the street corner for him to emerge. She considered walking back and knocking on his front door. If he was in there and didn't want to come out, then she wasn't going to bother him. Once she was officially late for school, she walked on, alone.

She stopped at the main office to sign the tardy book. It was a simple, black, spiral-bound notebook just like the one Donnie was using when his father killed himself. Megan recalled that black notebook and the ominous things written in it. The terrible thought that Donnie hadn't made it through the night occurred to her for the first time. Donnie may not have walked to school because he may not have been alive.

She was angry at herself for letting him drive off without discussing it yesterday. She was disappointed that she didn't go back to knock on his door to check on him that morning. Megan began to cry again for the hundredth time since breaking the news to Donnie the previous day.

The administrative assistant who was preparing Megan's tardy slip to take to class noticed. "Megan," she said, "are you all right, honey?"

Megan nodded.

"Is something wrong at home?"

"No." Megan's one word came out in a blubbery mess.

"What is it?"

Megan responded by crying some more.

"Honey," the assistant said, "why don't you sit down right there for a minute?"

Megan plopped down in a yellow, plastic stationary seat. She was oblivious to the action of the office and the occasional staring student.

"Megan, come on with me." Mrs. Griffith, one of the school's counselors, was sitting next to her. Her words came out like puffs of cotton, "We'll get you some water and a few tissues so you can go to class."

Mrs. Griffith stood and Megan's body did the same without her brain telling it to.

It was the first time she had ever been in Mrs. Griffith's office. It was a very confined room with dark yellow walls and fake wood furniture. Instead of sitting behind her desk, the school counselor sat in the seat next to Megan.

When Megan calmed down, Mrs. Griffith ventured a question, "Do you want to tell me what's wrong?"

Megan simplified her concerns, "I'm moving."

"Ohhhh," Mrs. Griffith was sympathetic. Recalling what brought Megan to Haviland High a year ago, the counselor asked, "Did your father get a new job?"

"Promotion." She had stopped crying, but her sniffles wouldn't go away. "I don't want to go. I don't want to leave my friends…"

"I know. I know." Mrs. Griffith's voice was soothing. "It's hard starting over."

"And over and over and over…" Megan complained. "And this time…"

Megan paused for a long time. Mrs. Griffith waited. Megan thought the counselor would verbally prompt her to say more, but she didn't. After a minute of silence, Megan spoke again. "This time, I'm leaving behind someone who means a lot to me and… and he's hurt… I've hurt him. I didn't mean to, but I have. I didn't mean to…" Megan's tears started again. Her words came out in breathy sobs. "I didn't know we were moving again. I thought for sure this was home, that this was it. I like it here. I wouldn't have done it. I wouldn't have… I didn't mean to hurt him…"

Avoiding particulars that Megan might not want to provide, Mrs. Griffith inquired, "Is he a student at this school?"

Megan inhaled deeply through her nose and answered the counselor, "He is Donnie Betts."

Mrs. Griffith offered a sympathetic smile and gently patted Megan on the back. She was careful not to let Megan see the worry that raced through her. Donnie had spent a lot of time in the exact chair in which Megan sat. Other than that mishap at the very beginning of the school year, he seemed to be progressing and adjusting to life after his father's suicide. Now, she understood why. Donnie had found someone. Donnie managed to love again and now for the second time in his short life, he was losing a loved one. To say that Mrs. Griffith wasn't worried would have been a lie.

To add to her distress, Megan informed her that Donnie didn't come to school.

Mrs. Griffith told Megan that she would call the Betts's to see if Donnie was OK.

"Can you do it now?" Megan asked. "While I'm here?"

"No. I want you to go to class. I'll take care of your tardiness today and give you a pass to get into class. The best thing for you to do is go on with your day. Worrying about it won't change anything. Do something with yourself. Do something productive today. OK?"

Megan nodded. She stayed until lunch before she ducked out. The mattress was being delivered between noon and three. Someone had to be there when it arrived.

She wished that Donnie would already be there. Perhaps he slept in and then decided to skip school altogether and go straight to the storage unit to meet the furniture truck. No such luck.

The garage door was down and locked, just as she had left it.

She went inside and waited for the deliverymen who arrived before one o'clock. They asked her if she lived in the storage unit and why she needed the mattress.

Megan was indignant. "No. And it's none of your business." She signed her name on the paperwork and they left.

She pulled the garage door down. Using the new sheets, she made the bed and curled up on it. Despite the bed's comfort, it didn't feel right without Donnie. This was something they were supposed to share. They were supposed to recline on it while listening to audio books. Donnie was supposed to play his guitar on it while Megan finished her homework. Megan was supposed to rest on it after a shift at Friendly's while Donnie wrote in his notebook. She was not supposed to be lying on it alone.

This helped her understand some of Donnie's pain. In a few weeks, it would be he who was alone in the storage unit.

When it was late enough for her to go home without arousing suspicion, she closed and locked the storage unit's door.

Megan's face was sore from crying. It felt puffy and tight from the dried tears. The combination of leaving Haviland

and hurting Donnie upset her more than she had even been.

Her walk home was slow and pathetic. Her feet scraped along the sidewalk as her eyes examined the cracks therein.

Mrs. Griffith told her that she would call the Betts's to check on Donnie, but Megan wanted to see for herself. If she went home for the evening without attempting to see Donnie, she wouldn't be able to stop thinking about all of the things that may have gone wrong with him.

She pushed the Betts's doorbell. Suddenly impatient, she pushed it a second time. The door creaked open a mere foot.

"Hi, Mrs. Betts," Megan said, flashing her forged smile. Only Donnie could tell the difference between that one and the authentic thing.

"Megan. Hi." Mrs. Betts appeared somewhat listless.

"Donnie wasn't at school today. Is he all right?"

"He's not feeling well today."

"Oh." Megan brightened somewhat. She didn't want Donnie to have a cold or the flu, but it would be better than wallowing in self-depression or worse. "What's wrong?"

"Well, Megan, sometimes people don't feel well physically and sometimes they don't feel well because of other things and Donnie's just having a bad day."

"Oh." Megan's initial instincts were accurate. "Um... Can I see him?" She had never been inside the Betts's household.

"I think that he's better off left alone, right now."

Megan disagreed. She played with the latch on her satchel while trying to think of what to say that might get her inside.

"I appreciate your concern," Mrs. Betts told Megan. "I'll let him know that you stopped by. Maybe tomorrow he will be feeling better."

"I hope." She didn't want to leave without giving Mrs. Betts a message from her to him. She wanted Donnie to remember how much he meant to her. "Could you tell him something for me? Please tell him that I listened to the Ramones all day." It wasn't the truth, but Donnie would understand her message.

"I'll tell him for you. Goodbye." The door closed.

TWENTY-SIX

Two days later, Donnie returned to school. He avoided walking with Megan by taking his bike. She didn't even know that he was there until she saw him in their third period Chemistry class. She could hardly wait until class was over to speak with him.

After the bell rang, she rushed over to Donnie. They always walked to study hall together.

When Donnie turned right out of the classroom instead of left, Megan said, "Miss a few days and forget where you're going? Study hall is this way."

He barely looked at her. "I have a test to make up from Monday."

Megan didn't see him again until lunch. He still sat at the same table as Dale. No one there minded having him at the table, but it was obvious that Donnie was in no mood to speak. They didn't try to include him in their conversation.

Megan had to talk with him. Leaving her uneaten lunch, she walked over to Donnie's table.

Standing above him, she asked, "Can I talk to you over there?" She pointed to some lockers near the student store.

Donnie paid her little attention, "I'm eating lunch right now."

"Donnie!"

Reluctantly, he stood and followed her.

She knew that there were a lot of eyes on them and didn't want to make a scene. She tugged lightly and indiscreetly at the bottom of his long-sleeved, yellow T-shirt.

"I'm sorry, Donnie. I don't want to move. Do you understand that? I don't want to leave Haviland. I don't want to leave you."

"But, you are." The pain in his voice was evident to Megan. She hated hearing it.

"I'll email you. I'll call."

"It's not the same. Plus, you won't call. You won't write."

"Yes, I will, Donnie."

"Just like you kept in touch with your friends from the school before this one?" Donnie remembered the photo she kept in her bedroom. The one in which she wore the jean jacket and her hair was a bland brown with a boring cut. When he asked about the girls in the picture, Megan had told him that they were from her old school and she didn't stay in contact with them after she moved.

"You're different," she said.

"It's not like you're moving to a different school and I'll still see you at football games. You're moving to a state that's a thousand miles away."

She couldn't look at his face. It was too hard. No one else in the school might notice the pain smeared across it, but she saw it. Looking toward their feet, she said, "I can't help it that we're moving. I wanna make the most of our time left together."

"Why? Just to make it harder on me? So I can remember all the fun we had when I'm left here alone? I don't think so. Memories aren't worth anything." He would know.

"Please Donnie. At least meet me at Unit #143. We got the mattress on Monday. I was there when it was delivered."

"I can't. I have to work. I haven't been in in days. Dirt's gotta be furious."

"He is."

"How do you know?"

"I was there yesterday. Looking for you."

"Stop looking for me!" When anger rose up in Donnie, he became a scary individual. "It's over. You're leaving."

"Not 'til Sunday."

"Sunday? I thought you said a month?"

"My mom already found a house." Megan hated breaking even more bad news to him. "This is my last week at Haviland High. Everything is going so fast."

Donnie stared at the girl who made it possible for him to love again. His life was hardly worth living before she came along. Television was boring. The radio was dull. Going to school was a chore. Talking was overrated. Megan turned all of that around for him. He learned that he was able to get out of life as much as he put in. But, this was unfair.

"Please, Donnie," Megan said. "Please. I don't want it to end like this. Meet me at the storage unit."

"Megan, I'm going back to my table now."

"No, please."

"I'm going back to my table. I'm sorry that I can't give you full credit for ruining my life, but it was pretty much already destroyed when you got here."

"Don't go."

"Don't go? That's what I should be saying to you."

"Donnie…"

"I'm going back to my table. All right? Leave me alone." He pulled her hand from his shirt and rejoined his lunch table. He knew that it was somewhat irrational to be angry with her because it wasn't her fault they were moving, but he couldn't help the way he felt.

Donnie used work as an excuse not to meet with Megan later that day, but it wasn't a lie. He went straight to the driving range after school.

8 *Christopher Cleary*

"Well, look who decided to come back to work," Dirt said when Donnie pulled around the corner on his bike. "You've got to give me your number kid. You disappear and I can't get hold of you? Them golf balls started piling up. You know I had to go out there and pick them up myself?"

Donnie felt bad about that. He got along well with Dirt and didn't mean to leave him without help for a few days. "Sorry, Dirt."

"Sorry my butt. Where've you been?"

"Trying to get right."

It was easy to tell that Donnie was more somber than usual. Dirt usually hated this trait in teenagers, but recognized that he was a good kid who caught a few lousy breaks. He picked up on it because he had been one himself. This made Dirt uncharacteristically sympathetic to Donnie's situation.

Since he had an image to maintain, Dirt disguised his concern by asking, "Whatever is bothering you, you better get it out. I'm not paying you to mope around out there in slow motion. So, what is it?"

"Nothing. I'm fine."

"Like Hell." Dirt thought of his girlfriend with the pretty hair who came by the day before. "Oh Donnie, don't tell me it's the girl. Tell me it's anything but something with that girl." Dirt wasn't equipped with the knowledge to help with girl problems, but then again, few guys were.

Donnie didn't reply. He put on his batting helmet and got ready to pick up golf balls.

"Oh man, it's the girl, ain't it?" Dirt scratched one of his hairy arms with one of his hairy hands. "C'mon, sit down. I'll buy you a soda."

Donnie heard the side door of the shack with the saltbox roof bang shut. Following that was the sound of two soda cans rattling to the bottom of the vending machine.

They sat down together on the bench. Dirt ripped open his can of cola, took a giant gulp, and let a huge belch rip. A number of golfers looked his way. "You ain't on the PGA Tour and there ain't no guys holding up 'Quiet' signs," Dirt yelled at them. "Back to what you're doing!" They resumed hitting golf balls. He looked at his can and frowned. "I should probably be drinking diet." He took another swig and leaned back. "OK Donnie, lay it on me."

Donnie was unsure if he wanted to discuss it with anyone, but if he had to, there were worse options than Dirt. "Her dad got a promotion, so they're moving."

"Where?"

"To Pennsylvania."

"Unless you got a ton of frequent flyer miles saved up, that's a problem."

"I don't."

"I figured."

They both paused to take a drink.

"This will be her third school since she started high school," Donnie said. "It's a pattern. Why would she get involved with me when she knows that she's just gonna move out of my life? Why would she do that to me? It makes me mad."

"It ain't her fault she's moving. Sounds like her dad is the one with problems. Seems like he's trying to find happiness through his work instead of his family. I'm the same way."

"Really?"

"Hell no. I work in a shack, for crying out loud. What I'm saying is, there's no point being mad at the girl."

"But she's ditching me."

"She ain't ditchin' you, Donnie. People's paths come together and go apart. That's the way it is."

"It stinks."

"You gonna be working here when you're thirty?"

"I hope not."

"That's like you're ditchin' me, then. See? You should be happy for what time you guys had."

"I thought we'd have more of it."

"What do you do when things don't work out the way you plan? I'm askin' you. What do you do?"

"What do you mean?"

"C'mon now. I know everything hasn't gone perfect for you. What do you do when something unplanned comes up?"

A new customer walked in from the parking lot. He looked inside the shack to see if anyone was there. When he realized it was empty, he said to Dirt, "Excuse me..."

"Yeah?" Dirt asked, somewhat rude to his patron.

"Where's the manager?"

"You're looking at him!"

"Oh," the man was taken aback. He didn't expect the owner to be a street urchin. "I would like a large bucket of golf balls, please."

"All right. Here," Dirt extended his hand, "gimme five bucks and grab a bucket. Sheesh!" The man handed Dirt five singles from his wallet. Dirt closed his hand around the bills and shoved them in his pocket.

"It makes me feel miserable," Donnie said. "Like I got nothing else."

"No one person should be your whole life, kid. You've got to be yourself and let others be a part of your life, not make them your life. What do you do when you're not with her?"

"I don't know. Nothing."

"C'mon, you do something."

"I read. Um, play guitar. Ride my bike. Drink Polar Slurps. Play arcade games. Pick up golf balls." He left out telling Dirt that he wrote down his thoughts in a notebook. He thought that a tough fellow like Dirt might find that wimpy.

"There you go. You still got all that."

"None of it matters if I don't have Megan."

Dirt blew out a long breath. "Donnie, you make me happy I never had kids."

Donnie finished off his can of soda. "Believe me. They're just as lucky."

TWENTY-SEVEN

Donnie disliked riding his bike to and from school, but he did it for the remainder of the week to avoid Megan.

The rest of her friends, especially Sada and the girls at her lunch table, tried to make her final week at Haviland High special and memorable. During Friday's lunch, they held a mini-going away party for her. It came complete with cone hats, noisemakers (which were confiscated by the teachers on cafeteria duty), and several disposable cameras. She appreciated all of it. It was nice to know that she would be missed, but all she really wanted was some alone time with Donnie.

After her last day at Haviland High, Megan waited for Donnie by his bike. He saw her through the windows and paused to see if she would give up and leave after a minute or two. She smiled and waved to her friends as they got on their busses and walked to their cars. It was clear that the cutie in the afternoon sun had no intentions of leaving her post.

He didn't want to talk to her. Donnie couldn't start forgetting about her soon enough. She might say a few things to him, but before she had a chance to say too much or hurt him even more, he'd be gone. The wheels of his bike would whip him away in a hurry. He pushed the door open and went outside.

"Hi, Donnie!" Megan sounded unusually chipper compared to the past few times they spoke.

"Hey, Megan." Donnie didn't let her enthusiasm suck him into a conversation. He just had to make it through the weekend and this episode of his life would be behind him.

"How was your day?" Still cheerful.

"Sucked." He got on his bike. When he did, he immediately figured out why Megan was so merry. He gave her a sidelong glance.

Megan's eyebrows bounced up and down twice.

She had deflated his tires.

Donnie dismounted and began pushing his bike. Megan followed alongside him.

Donnie said, "You're not going to ask if it's OK to walk with me?"

"Nope."

Together, they traveled the same path that they had walked several times over. Each silently took in the sights, sounds, and feel of this final walk together. It would be the last time the Richies' dog barked at them from the other side of its fence. They wouldn't get another chance to poke fun at New Hope Church's silly weekly sayings on its marquee. It was the last time they would pass Swifts together.

Megan thought about how she would never see these sights again. Donnie dwelled on viewing them every day but without Megan. Both knew they would miss being together.

Megan halted in front of Swifts. She said, "Can we stop here?" She spoke like it was her dying wish. "Please, Donnie."

"Sure, I need to get air in my tires."

She smiled at him. "Yeah, funny how you lost all the air out of both tires."

"Yeah, real funny."

Megan jumped in front of his bike. "K. Wait."

"What?"

"Promise me that you won't ride off as soon as you get air."

Megan Priddy was wearing a navy blue skirt with knee-high stockings. Her top was a warm and cozy gray sweater. Her magnificent trademark hair was styled in pig tails, something only she could get away with. Megan looked so hot that Donnie forgot that she was moving and that he was mad at her. He agreed to wait.

"Boffo!" Megan was excited. She ran inside the store without a worry that Donnie might ride off. Their relationship may have been under a strain lately, but she knew that Donnie would never break a promise.

He filled his tires with air and went inside to find Megan. She was standing in front of the soda fountain. Her arms were filled with packages of candies and cakes. "I want all this!" she exclaimed.

"What are you going to do with it?"

"Eat it!"

"All of it?"

"With your help." She saw that he wasn't sharing her excitement. She got closer to him. "See, Donnie. Wasn't our walk down Memory Lane nice? It was just a nice, pleasant walk without any bullshit. We can still have fun together. We're still Donnie and Megan. Nothing changes until Sunday morning."

"What happens then?... With us?"

She stood on her tiptoes and, slightly crushing the food between their bodies, kissed him on the lips. "Sunday is so far away."

The kiss made time stand still and Donnie responded, "Yeah, I guess it is."

Her lips curled back in a smile. "Here," she said, shoving the goodies into his arms, "hold this." She reached into her satchel and yanked out Donnie's discarded Pirates hat. "It's still too warm out for your ski mask," she said and fitted the baseball hat over his shaggy black hair. "You'll need this a while longer."

"Thanks."

"No sweat." She turned and went to work filling two large, sixty-four ounce cups with Sour Apple Polar Slurps.

"Those cups are for soda. They're too big for – "

Megan threw her head back and laughed, "I don't care."

If Donnie's hands weren't full, he would have scratched his head.

They dumped their booty of snacks and drinks from Swifts on the card table in Unit #143.

"That's a lot of crap," Donnie said, contemplating if he'd vomit from eating his half of it.

"Ohhhh yeah!" Megan ripped open a package of cupcakes. "I wish your guitar was here. I want to hear you play."

"I'll bring it tomorrow. I've sort of been working on something special."

"Really? Like what?"

"Like you'll see tomorrow."

She washed down her first bite of cupcake and said, "Well, I've got a surprise, too!"

"Oh, do you now?"

"That's right." That's wrong. She didn't. She was just playing and having fun. Still, she could come up with a surprise for Donnie by the next day. "Come on," she said, taking his hand. "Stand over here." She guided him to the wall with her chalk outline. She began to manipulate his limbs. His body was very stiff. Standing on her toes, she got close to his ear and whispered, "Relax, Donnie." A warm tremor rippled through his body when she kissed his neck. His body loosened. "That's better," she told him.

She had fun positioning his arms, legs, and head. She moved him into some very strange and awkward positions for her own amusement before settling on a simple one. Megan had Donnie stand next to her outline. She placed his hand directly over the outline of her waist-high hand.

"Hold still," Megan told him.

She tried going slow. She tried to take her time and revel in the joy of tracing Donnie's body, but she couldn't help herself. She loved it too much. Up and down his long legs. Around his lanky arms. She had to stand on a chair to do his head. With the chair's assistance, she was almost too tall and had to reach down to trace him.

Donnie commented, "You've gotten bigger."

"Yeah, I should try out for the basketball team."

"That's not what I meant."

Megan glanced down and saw that her chest was level with his gray eyes. She jumped down off the chair. With one hand on a hip and her other arm extended, she wagged her finger and admonished him, "Donnie Betts, shame on you."

She moved the chair and finished the chalk outline of her boyfriend. "There!"

Donnie stepped back and admired her work. "Very nice," he commented.

"See," Megan said, pointing to their outlines. "I made it so we're holding hands."

"That's cool."

"Yeah!" She bounded onto their new bed. "Have you tried out the bed yet?"

"No."

She positioned herself closer to the wall and made room for him. "Now would be a good time."

Donnie rolled onto the bed and they stared at the ceiling.

"We should put that Ramones poster up there," Megan commented.

Donnie was distracted. "This thing is more comfortable than my bed at home."

"It's the sheets." Megan was proud of her high thread count sheets.

"How could it be the sheets? I'm fully dressed."

Megan propped up on one arm. "And why is that?"

"Don't start, Megan," he warded her off. "We need to save something for tomorrow."

"Fine." She jumped off the mattress and sat down at the table.

"You didn't have to get out."

"Yeah, I did. The last thing I need to do is fall asleep and wander home at five in the morning."

"True." Donnie pulled his hands behind his head and tried not to think about what he would do after Megan was gone.

A n hour before they were to meet at the street corner to walk to Unit #143 for the last time, Donnie and Megan were individually making preparations to see the other.

Once out of the shower, both of them stood in front of their underwear drawers for a long time, contemplating which pair to put on. It could be the first time that someone of the opposite sex saw them.

Donnie purchased new jeans for the occasion. He had needed them for a while, but had been procrastinating going to the mall to buy them. Before he left the mall, he spotted a plaid, button-down shirt and purchased it without trying it on. In the safety of his own bedroom, he put it on with his new denims. After a long exhalation, he did the unthinkable – he tucked the shirt in. "Need a belt…" He walked out of his bedroom and went into his mother's room. Most of his father's clothing had been donated to charity, but Donnie knew a few belts had been left behind. He threaded the belt through the loops of his jeans and checked out his reflection in his mother's full-length mirror.

He turned his attention to his disheveled hair. His goal was to keep it messy enough that it didn't look like he worked on it very long, but neat enough that it looked stylish. Ironically, it took a very long time to achieve the effortless look he was going for.

Megan tried on and ripped off several different outfits. She wanted to look perfect for Donnie. If this was to be the last time he saw her live and in person, she wanted to be nothing less than a stunning sight for him to behold and never forget. Megan stood in front of her open closet that usually had endless possibilities of clothing. She was outgrowing her favorite items and the rest appeared drab. "Hmmm." Maybe she should pick out her shoes first? Aha! Boots. Big black boots that traveled up her calf and had a nice heel. In a way, they were practical, too, because Donnie was a rather tall boy. "K. Boots and... boots and... boots and what...?" she asked herself. "Just boots? Nah, too cold." She reached inside her closet and pulled out a deep rose-colored, velvet skirt that came down to the top of her boots. "Yes. And..." She slid a few tops back and forth before removing a black as her boots thin wool top adorned with large black buttons. "Got it."

After she dressed, Megan twisted and turned in the mirror, trying to view herself from all sides. Using an aristocratic English accent, she complimented the girl in the mirror, "Darling, you look smashing. Simply smashing." She painted her nails a dark red to match her skirt and let her hair run wild down her shoulders.

Donnie brushed his teeth. Twice. The Betts's medicine cabinet was a plastic box kept under the sink. During the second brushing, he rifled through the box and pulled out a few of the items. He tossed them in his backpack along with his notebooks.

Back in front of the mirror, Megan turned her head from side to side. The features of her face did not appear symmetrical. She took turns facing left and then right, looking at herself through the corners of her eyes and then quickly turning to see if the opposite side of her face matched. After a half dozen of these whiplash maneuvers, she looked at herself dead on in the mirror and said, "That's got to be your imagination."

She called Donnie a few minutes before he was about to walk out of his house to meet her at the street corner.

"I got the van," she told him. "I'll be there in a minute."

"Can't we just walk?" Donnie asked.

"I've been packing all day and haven't eaten a thing since breakfast. We need to get some food, stat. I'm starving."

"Sit down? Drive-thru? Take out?"

"I don't care." She didn't give Donnie a chance to respond. "I'm hanging up, grabbing my satchel, and backing out of my driveway and into yours. Bye." Click.

Donnie watched from his bedroom window. Sure enough, the van backed out of the Priddys' driveway and into his. Megan held the horn down just in case he had fallen asleep during the thirty seconds that passed since she last spoke with him.

Donnie opened the sliding door of the blue van and set down his guitar, tossed his backpack in next to Megan's satchel, and got in the passenger seat next to her.

She asked, "Pizza?"

"I just had that for lunch yesterday."

"Oh yeah. Pizza on Fridays." She put a few fingers to her forehead. "I always forget that. I guess that I don't have to try to remember anymore."

"How about Chinese?"

"Great. I'm so hungry I could eat a panda."

They got Chinese take-out and brought it back to Unit #143. They shoved the snacks left over from the previous day aside and spread out their array of Chinese splendor on the card table.

"I love egg rolls," Donnie said before proceeding to eat them like French fries.

"Hey! Save one for me. Would ya?"

When a good portion of the food was gone, they slouched back in their chairs.

"Fortune cookie time," Donnie said, shoving one her way and picking up one for himself.

Each of them cracked open their cookies. Megan pulled her slip of paper out and read it to herself. "Mine's pretty good," she said.

Donnie was perplexed. He looked from one half of his cookie to the other. He broke the halves into smaller pieces.

"What's wrong?" Megan asked.

"I don't have one."

"You didn't get a fortune?"

"No." Donnie stared at the crumbs of his fortune cookie in bewilderment. "What does that mean?"

"I don't know. It's weird. I can tell you that." She reviewed her sliver of paper. "You wanna hear mine?"

"Huh?" he looked up from the mess he had made. "Yeah, all right."

"K…" she read her fortune from the strip of paper, "'New delights are old delights that you've forgotten about.' Actually, that's not good."

"At least you got one."

They did the dishes by putting all of their empty wrappers and containers in a plastic trash bag and setting it outside of the unit, near the van. Donnie pulled his guitar out of the vehicle before they returned inside.

When Megan saw this, she plopped down on the bed and said, "Donnie Betts, are you going to serenade me?"

"Um…," he strummed a few chords on the guitar. Turning the knobs at the end of its long neck, he fiddled with it until it was properly tuned.

"I remember when it took you an hour just to tune that thing," she said.

"I'm not that much better."

"Yes, you are."

He practiced through a few chords that he would be using in the song. "OK. I'm ready."

Megan's feet hung off the bed. Her hands were in her lap, making a small depression in the deep rose-colored, velvet skirt. She sat upright and attentive.

The song began with a few introductory notes immediately followed by quick repetitive riffs. The music resonated off the walls of the storage unit.

He sang:

Got all I need
When I had you
Had some wants
But just a few

Whisked me away
To a new mood
Then threw me back
To my solitude

Donnie altered the chords and played them at a punchy pace for the chorus. His voice sailed overtop of them.

Now you're gone
Like fallen leaves
Ain't nothin' left
But memories

He returned to the regular rhythm of the verse.

Don't offer me

A lock o' your hair
Remembering you
Is too much to bear

Quick again and nearly screaming for the second chorus.

Now you're gone
Like fallen leaves
Ain't nothin' left
But memories

Then calmly. Gentler and lighter strokes than the previous verses.

They ain't much
They do me no good
But cause me pain
I knew they would

He closed the song by repeating the same notes that he opened with.

TWENTY-NINE

Megan was blown away by Donnie's one-song concert.

In public, Donnie dodged most attention. He never felt comfortable when the focus was on him. It got easier every day, but he had difficulties shaking the anxiety and shame associated with his father's suicide. He vowed never to hide from who he was or his past, but he wasn't ready to make himself available for examination by everyone. He loosened up around Megan, but there were still times when he kept to himself.

Donnie exhibited zero inhibitions during his performance. It reminded Megan of when he practiced his oral presentation. When he wanted to, Donnie Betts was able to let go. He was able to turn himself into a great orator, or, in this case, a rock star. He released his emotions and committed to the piece. Watching him play was like opening up one of his notebooks.

The acoustic guitar was Donnie's magic wand. When he was done and leaned it against the wall, his powers dissipated. He went from outgoing to somewhat shy again.

"Good?" he inquired.

"Donnie that was…," she tucked a lock of peach-toned hair behind her ear, "That was really good."

"Yeah?" Donnie didn't appear excited about her compliment. "One of these days, I'll get an electric. It will sound way better then. It's not exactly an unplugged type of song."

Megan held her hands up, chest high, palms facing Donnie. "I'm not expressing myself good enough. Donnie, that song, it's like mega-boffo. It could be on the radio." She cocked her head to one side and lowered her eyebrows, "Did you get it from the radio?"

"No. I wrote it. Are you putting me on?"

"No! Not at all. I want you to play it again." She clapped her hands lightly a few times.

"Maybe later."

She crossed her arms. "And it's not like it's a good depiction of me. You kind of make me sound cruel in it... But still, it is totally kick ass! I didn't know you could play that well or sing like that."

"Me, neither," he said, running a free hand through his hair. "I guess I'm better at writing songs than learning ones that already exist."

"And the way you perform. You totally throw yourself into it. You're gone. You're in the moment. Your commitment to the song is amazing. It's great. How do you do it?"

Donnie sat down and swallowed a gulp of soda. Like a rock star reluctantly giving an interview, Donnie scanned the floor with his eyes and considered his answer. "I think maybe, for me, it's like reading fiction. It's not real. I can trick myself into thinking that I'm someone else. I'm pretending..."

"No, you're not." She looked at Donnie through new eyes. "That's you, Donnie. I know you."

Donnie shrugged. "I guess that maybe, singing is just easier than saying."

It was a revelation for both of them. They shared a smile at having made this connection.

Megan added, "And you're totally hot!" She jumped up from the mattress and sat on his lap, her body facing his.

"You should play it in the spring talent show." She threw her head back. "That's a great idea!" she exclaimed, whipping her head back down. Her scrumptious hair flew everywhere. "Do it and tape it for me. The school has a digital video camera. Get a copy and email it to me!"

"I don't know, Megan."

"You've got talent. You really have a knack for being in front of people and entertaining." Her excitement transformed into wonderment. "It's so strange because... Because you don't look like it. You look introverted and afraid of expression, but really... You're deliciously amazing. You're this astonishing person who is sincere and so real." She took a deep breath in and slowly exhaled. "And I know that inside, you feel tortured, but you're not afraid. You're not. You have this strength that no one has a clue about. Some magical strength that you keep secret and use only when you need it. God, you're unbelievable."

Donnie became so incredibly irresistible that Megan suddenly couldn't keep her lips off him. Supporting her behind with his hands, Donnie stood and carried her to the mattress. Their mouths barely came apart during the transition.

Shoes were kicked off. Megan's shirt was flung away. When she went to remove Donnie's, she was nearly too out of breath to joke, "All you ever wear are hoodies, but you pick today to wear a shirt with buttons."

Things happened in a slow flurry. Kisses interspersed the removal of clothing. They tried to take off each other's garments, but some articles were just easier to do themselves. They were too busy admiring the other person's body to be insecure about their own. The trust they had established allowed a charming vulnerability. When they were stripped down to next to nothing, they had never felt closer. The sensations, the experience was exhilarating.

"Now for my surprise," Megan said.

She tip-toed around the storage unit blowing out candles wearing little more than her skirt.

She dragged her satchel toward the mattress and sat back down. From it, she produced a strip of condoms. The only other time she had held them in her hand was when she "borrowed" her sister's driver's license to illegally rent the storage unit. They were in her purse at the time. That's where Megan got her courage to purchase them herself.

The remainder of their clothing was caringly taken from their bodies.

Over the course of a year, their relationship had progressed to that moment. It was time. They were ready for sex.

At first, their minds interfered. They had certain ideas of how the first time was supposed to be. The results were awkward and clumsy.

Donnie whispered, "I think we're trying too hard."

They slowed down and relaxed, allowing their bodily instincts to take over.

Their five senses were fully stimulated: The visual beauty of each other. The taste of each others lips and flesh. The tiny breeze of breath against skin. The mixture of perfume and sweat. Only the sound of the quiet rhythms between their bodies.

It ended with a bolt of bliss that paralyzed their bodies and lingered long after they were done.

Donnie stroked her cheek with the back of his hand and asked in a low voice, "Was it what you'd thought it would be?"

"Yes and no."

"How would you describe it?"

"It's so pure and so unique, that I think it can only be described as the act itself."

"Yeah."

She took his hand and kissed it. "For some reason," she said, "I thought my life would be totally different after I had sex…"

"But it's not…"

"No."

"I know what you mean." Then Donnie noticed something for the first time. "Wow. You're right. These sheets are really comfortable."

"Told ya."

THIRTY

The warm breath on his ear stirred his slumber more than the gentle voice whispering his name, "Donnie… Donnie."

"What time is it?" he muttered, not wanting to shift his body for fear that his beautiful dream would disappear.

"After midnight," Megan whispered to him. "I have to go."

Megan had relit a few of the candles. He noticed that, unlike him, she was dressed.

"Nooo," he moaned softly.

"I'm sorry, Donnie. I don't want to."

They had discussed their potential future and it was bleak. The telephone and email were two ways to keep in touch. Snail mail was even an option. In the end, they agreed that none of them would work. It was nearly impossible for two high school teenagers to carry on a relationship that stretched over seven-hundred miles. It would have been difficult for most adults. There was no way that it could work for them. In the end, they reluctantly accepted it. Their paths met at a tangent and now they were separating. The Donnie Betts and Megan Priddy Experience was coming to a close.

The storage unit was paid in full for nearly three months in advance. At that time, Donnie would either have to switch it to his name or vacate. He didn't know what he would do. He neither wanted to come back to Unit #143 without his girlfriend nor did he want to let go of it.

"I wish you didn't have to go," Donnie told her.

"Me, too." Quiet tears followed the contour of her cheeks. "Nothing is forever."

She bent over so they could kiss goodbye. It was soft and gentle. Both tried hard to memorize it.

"I love you, Donnie Betts."

"I love you, too."

She moved away from the bed and threw her satchel across her body. Megan grudgingly lifted the garage door. The security lights of Parkside Storage mixed with the moonlight and shone into the storage unit. Donnie turned to look and saw Megan's silhouette standing in the doorway. Her arm reached up and took hold of the door. Slowly, she began to disappear from him forever. First, her head and peach-colored locks, followed by her upper body and torso. Then her waist, hips, and thighs – all gone forever. Finally all he could see was a glimmer of light reflecting off her shiny black boots and then they were gone, too.

Donnie rolled over and went back to sleep. This time it was a dark depression that overwhelmed him and not the dreamy comfort of holding that special someone.

The windowless storage unit felt like a jail cell when he woke. He was groggy. It was impossible for him to know the time. The overhead light was off. The candlelight of the few lit candles flickered on the concrete walls. Nakedness left him feeling cold. He pulled on his jeans and shirt before his eyelids came down and he dozed off again.

The next time they opened, his heart felt like an empty carton of milk, crushed and discarded. The insides of his body moaned in pain. Picking up the pieces of his life seemed like such a chore. They were scattered everywhere, most of them shattered into tiny shards. And too many of them were lost, never to be found again. It was impossible for his life to be complete.

His body felt weighed down like it was carrying a thousand golf balls. Again it moaned from the inside. This time louder. His nose began to tingle and he felt the slight sting of salty tears fill his eyes. Donnie took a large breath to try to calm himself, but it was like adding oxygen to the fire burning inside him. He knew the best cure for this was more sleep. Delightful sleep. Everything was OK while he slept. Exhausted from crying, he drifted off again.

The next time he came to, Donnie scooped a bottle of water from the floor and sat down at the card table with his back to the Ramones poster. Other than a few of the three-wick candles, the room had no light. It was very dim.

Donnie Betts couldn't conjure a reason to leave the storage unit ever again.

He shuffled things around in his backpack. Inside was every notebook he had ever filled. He left them there. Following the sounds of the rattling, his hands pulled out three plastic bottles of pills. One contained his mother's sleeping pills, another was filled with heavy pain medication left over from his wisdom teeth removal, and the third was unidentifiable. In the darkness, it was difficult to tell them apart and he didn't make the effort to ascertain which was which.

The skin beneath the scabs from his father's suicide had just begun the long healing process. Those scabs had been ripped off him and Donnie was bleeding again. It was so much blood that amputation was the only answer. He saw no reason to suffer any longer.

He lined up all three bottles in front of him. There was no way that he was going to screw this up. He would swallow down two of each every thirty seconds until they were gone. Soon after, it would all be over.

The one person, the single person that he cared for more than any other, had just left. He had felt abandoned by his father when he killed himself, but Donnie knew that no one would miss him when he was gone. Donnie wasn't going to kill himself to show everyone how much he meant or how much he would be missed. While he was awake, he suffered the constant battery of one thing after another that brought about memories of departed loved ones. When Donnie slept, he was unaware of that steady pain that flowed through his veins. Forget it all – no more heartache. Donnie was going to do it because he wanted to sleep forever.

He looked across the storage unit at the chalk outlines. There they were, hand in hand. The pain associated with seeing this affirmed that he was doing the right thing.

Pushing down and twisting, Donnie removed the caps from all three bottles and dumped their contents in three piles on the card table. Unit #143 was where he would die. He unscrewed the top of his water bottle.

Taking one last look at his and Megan's silhouettes on the wall, Donnie noticed something that wasn't there before. It was dark and he wasn't sure that his eyes were functioning properly. He tilted his head and rubbed his right eye. There were words written in chalk. He picked up a candle from the corner of the room and walked to the wall.

While he slept and before she left, Megan had written on the concrete blocks of the storage unit. There was a speech bubble like in comic strips coming from her mouth. She was saying: "Donnie Betts is my hero."

He read it again… and again… and again… and again… and again…

It read the same every time. "Donnie Betts is my hero."

His courage came creeping back. Megan loved him. She admired him. She found him to be inspirational. Donnie needed to be brave. He needed to go on. For her. For him. He was a survivor. He could achieve the unattainable. "Donnie Betts is my hero."

Everything changed.

He wanted to play his song again. He wanted to write more of them. He wanted to go to school. He wanted to get A's. Donnie wanted to share his strength with his mother and help create a better life for them. He wanted to see Dirt again and pick up golf balls at the driving range. He wanted to go golfing on a real golf course with his clubs. He wanted to ride his bike. He wanted to find love again. He wanted to show the world that he could face every adversity imaginable and overcome them all!

He yanked the door of the storage unit open. The morning sun forced him to squint, but he adjusted quickly to the glare.

The air was crisp and clean. The sun was warm and welcoming. Donnie stared up at the sky. The future was wide open.

He wanted breakfast. He wanted to taste pancakes and bacon on his tongue and savor their scrumptiousness.

He slung his guitar around him so it hung on his back and snatched his backpack off the card table. It, along with his notebooks of despair, would go in the dumpster on his way out.

The only other item that he took with him was a chewed-up purple pen of Megan's. He thought fondly of her and their time together. A piece of her would always be with him. They had built a love that would not die. And who knows, if he worked hard and got his grades up and studied for the SATs, he might end up at the same college as she. He slipped the pen in his back pocket.

There were endless possibilities awaiting him on the outside of Parkside Storage's fence.

Donnie Betts, the hero, looked over Unit #143 and pulled its door closed for the last time.

THE END

ABOUT THE AUTHOR

CHRISTOPHER CLEARY wrote scenes for talent shows in high school, plays in college, and a television pilot in Burbank, California. His undergraduate degree is in acting and his master's degree is in project management. He loves rocking out to Pearl Jam, rooting for the Steelers, and taking it easy with his wife and dog.